Wonder Lands
Are
Calling

A Max and Charles Nature Adventure
Book 6

SUSAN YARUTA-YOUNG

SECANT
PUBLISHING

Introduction

Wonder lands. Where are they? How to find them?

Wonder can be found anywhere. Listen. Look. Open your senses to all things around you. Then there is a good chance you'll discover wonderment in places you once thought were ordinary.

You don't need to follow a pocket watch–carrying white rabbit down a garden path or enter a backwards world through a "looking glass." Wind-filled willows by riverbanks still offer magical escapes. By northern beaches, tidal pools wait to be found in granite ledges carved into watery hollows by the sea; here, at low tide, tiny villages fill with swirling miniature creatures— shrimp, periwinkles, hermit crabs—as sea stars hide behind draped rockweed. Secret gardens are discovered when robin songs lead seekers to rusty keys buried just trowel scrapes beneath rich earth.

Other lands appear when ticking time pauses between the first and last peals of old church clocks. Shadows, so it has been written, separate from their owners, choose other free-wheeling partners, and dance together on full-moon nights, hidden from crowds and locked safely behind fences in gated, public gardens.

Imagination is not like baby shoes or plastic sippy cups to be outgrown and stored away. No, imagination always waits for you to come back. It welcomes you with open arms. It invites you to be reintroduced to the person you thought you'd lost when graduating from nursery rhymes and Mother Goose to essays describing voyages the Beagle made across wild seas or, years later, rocket flights into darkest space. Great scientists, writers, musicians, painters—all will tell you they have never grown too old for imagination games.

There are millions and millions of worlds where wonderment happens when you begin to search. Wonderment happens when you visit a special place for the first time, but it is also rediscovered each time you begin to see through the eyes of someone who sees a place for the first time. When you share favorite nature worlds with others, you rediscover that what you once believed ordinary is, in fact, extra ordinary.

On May 31, 1987, wild May apples bloomed between forest hedgerows and moss-filled groves. In icy springs, white sand churned swirling-upward messages inscribed on black tatters of ancient leaves and twigs. They drifted free, away from deep aquifers, and escaped center earth to appear on surface calm. Rivers, lakes, and ponds filled with flutters, flashes, as fin-flicking brook trout surfaced, seeking hatches of tiny mayflies (or duns) floating on watery surfaces. Surrounding all, on this early morning, wind songs swept through new fully furled leaves, blending with crow caws, the mourning doves' haunting call, and a cicada chorus.

Max and Charles lived where all these nature experiences happened every day. They'd seen, heard, and wandered on the wonder land of "The Property" all their lives. It didn't seem unique to them.

May 31, 1987, was like many days they'd lived before. Then it happened. On this day, they shared their world with others, and as they did, they understood their "everyday" WAS actually special.

Later, as afternoon slunk into evening, new worlds opened before them. In a parklike place, inside Baltimore City's boundary lines, Max and Charles became THE ONES experiencing different wild wonder lands. They walked quiet, shaded sidewalks. The deepening darkness was lit by porch lights, lamps gleaming from family homes, and at each corner, street lights casting down spots of brightness. A destination became the pink warm glow of the city's first mall. Walking with new friends, they were surrounded by loud buzzing as the seventeen-year cicadas sang high-pitched songs of joy while flying in first, final flight adventures, hurtling wildly through the world of Roland Park.

Chapter 1

May 31, 1987
Saturday Morning Beams Bright,
Ending Night Dreams

Early dawn.

Outside, in places where land and woods had not been disturbed in the last seventeen years, a loud drumming surrounded everything.

Deep in earth burrows, among wildflower bulbs, tangled vines, and old tree roots, the cicadas had burrowed down and taken nourishment from woody juices. Then came the year when they knew it was time to begin climbing upward; their wait was ending. Over the last few years, they'd traveled through earthy burrows.

Spring 1987, and the cicadas' slow journey brought them to the world of light they'd left seventeen years before, a place where time is divided: days often filled with sun, black nights shiny with moonglow and stars.

Max and Charles lived with their family in a cedar-shingle house near the forest. Directly behind the house, a narrow "fence" of towering pine trees stretched for acres. Here, when sunrise colored the sky in yellows, oranges, and reds, the cicada song began.

Inside the Cape Cod house, sunlight brightened the bedroom thirteen-year-old Max shared with Charles, his ten-year-old brother. All was quiet. Max was sound asleep. He was enjoying a wondrous dream: Maine tidal pools filled with frisky hermit crabs skittering across stony sand and squeezing from one empty shell into the next. In this bay world, a mysterious girl with large brown eyes and long dark hair was humming incoming tide songs to a sleeping periwinkle she held in her hand. She was moving closer, about to bend down beside him.

"Hey, Max! Are you going to sleep all day? There's tons of stuff to do."

"Whawawa." Max pulled snuggly bedclothes over his head and tried to find the rocky Maine beach again, but it was fading. The dream images were waving, scratchy voices whispering, "Goodbye . . . until . . . next time we meet in . . . some . . . far . . . off . . . sleep . . ."

"Wake up, Max," Charles said again.

"Charles?" Max groaned. "Why are you awake? What is SO important you're up at dawn today?"

"Have you forgotten? The Maryland Fly Anglers Club will arrive at Grandpa and Grandma's soon. Today is the day Grandpa's trout graduate from their school in our hatchery pools. Today the club members will collect, count, and measure the trout, and then take them away, delivering them to their new home, Hunting Creek."

"Oh yeah, that's right. But, Charles, it happens every year," Max mumbled, still hoping to roll over and fall back into his great dream.

"Max! This year is different. The club is hosting fly-tying and fly-fishing lessons right HERE. Grandpa's friend, Mr. Burt, is coming to tell stories and draw wildlife sketches, and you know what a great storyteller he is! Remember? He tells a story and draws it at the same time? Someone else is bringing a grill. Grandma told me there's going to be all kinds of good eats. AND Fred said he knows at least two kids our age who are coming for part of the day. I mean, kids our age! Max! This is a first! We have to at least check out how cool or nerdy they are," Charles said, pulling on worn cutoffs and a faded T.

"Kids our age? Really? Well, hmm, that WOULD be a first," Max sighed. The dream had completely disappeared. He pushed off his bed covers.

"Yeah, and Fred said they live in Baltimore City. Think of it, they may never have experienced mucking through swamp mud or frog hunting, or crept up on a crayfish, or stuck a bloodworm onto a hook." Charles was digging through his closet for his oldest, smelliest, "holey-est," perfect-for-trout-collection-day sneakers.

"Charles, come on, you know if it's an event sponsored by the Maryland Fly Anglers, there won't be worms pierced on a hook but artificial flies that someone, most likely Grandpa, has made."

He pushed himself off the mattress, clumped onto the floor, and began searching for clothes that would be considered proper dress code for a special trout "goodbye, so long, maybe see you again someday" fly-fishing day, a day when other kids were maybe coming. It could be interesting. Over the last nine months, Max had begun to care about his appearance and how he dressed, unlike Charles, who still looked, dressed, smelled, and acted like a little kid.

"So when is stuff supposed to begin?"

"Mom said she's helping Grandma make a huge breakfast. If you inhale, you can smell . . ."

Max breathed in. "Ah!" he sighed, the fragrances of bacon frying, something sweet baking . . . rising from the kitchen, from room to room, until warm and cozy yumminess filled the air around them. "We'd better hurry and get ready, go downstairs, and see if we can help Mom. But, Charles, ugh, you'd better shower first." He sniffed his own armpits and added, "Me too."

"Why?"

"Just because, OK? Trust me. Just because," Max said.

Fifteen minutes later, at 6:35 a.m., both boys were clean, though damp, with wet hair combed by running fingers through it. They were dressed in detergent-scented clothes, arriving in the kitchen ready to help their mom.

"Wow. What great kids I have," Mom said, looking away from "tons" of bacon she was preparing. "I didn't even have to call for help, and here you are. Consider yourself air hugged . . . my hands are too busy. Drink your juice. Then there'll be sticky buns with your milk. I'll be taking them from the oven . . ."—she was hushed by the oven timer—"right now!" She grabbed a pot holder in one hand and opened the door to the steamy oven with the other, pulling out a cookie sheet lined with rows of caramel- and pecan-packed buns. She placed them on a hot plate, reached in again, and took out a second tray filled with cinnamon raisin rolls. With her hip, she closed the oven door.

"Is that all the baked goodies you've made?" Charles asked, counting. "Only a dozen of each kind, with members of the club plus guests coming?"

"Charles, don't be rude," Max said.

"Not to worry," said Mom. "Look what's on the dining room table."

The boys looked and saw many boxes full of sweet baked goods.

"But if we each have one, then you can't fill the last two boxes with a dozen of each kind," Charles said.

"It's OK. Grandma made five dozen more. You, Max, and yep, even your dear old mom will enjoy a sticky bun or cinnamon roll before the crowds appear." She looked at the wall clock. "But we must hurry. The first workers will arrive by seven."

Max, Charles, and Mom elbowed a space and, surrounded by boxes filled with sweets, enjoyed their yummy-but-hurried breakfast snack. A bigger, more relaxed breakfast would come later when Grandma was ready to serve the Maryland Fly Anglers members and friends.

After their snack, they rode with Mom in her van as she drove the fried bacon and many boxes of sweets down through the bumpy pony pasture and parked at the barn at Grandma and Grandpa's big house. They made numerous trips carrying in all the precooked food.

Long tables and folding chairs (borrowed from a local church) were set up under the shady oaks, between the cement porch and the stream that bubbled from the big spring and flowed through the trout pools and alongside and behind the house. The tables and chairs made Grandma and Grandpa's backyard look like a scene from *Alice in Wonderland*, before the Mad Hatter began serving his endless afternoon teas.

Grandma's kitchen was jammed and bustling like a restaurant, mall food court, or school cafeteria, as food preppers made varieties of breakfast delights: dozens of buns, cornbread and rolls, and pans of baked French toast. Fried scrapple, sausage, and bacon filled professional warming trays to the brim. Glass bowls overflowed with pale-green, orange, and bright-red melon balls. Everything was ready. Two institutional-sized coffee makers ("high-test" and decaf) burbled, sending coffee aromas through the room. Gallons of juice and milk— nestled in ice, wedged side by side in an old-fashioned zinc laundry tub—were already on the cement back porch and placed next to stacks of paper cups. When the club members and others arrived, the coffee would be moved outside and all drinks would be self-serve from the porch.

Helping in the kitchen was Mrs. Ellen, one of Grandma's friends. She was known far and wide as one the best fly-fishing women in the state. Her late husband, G., had been a famous Maryland fisherman and one of Grandpa's best friends.

Mrs. Ellen and Grandma greeted Mom and the boys with relief-filled smiles. "Glad you're here to help!"

Max and Charles looked at all the food. Their eyes grew wider, mouths dropped open, and tummies began to growl, making hungry noises even though they weren't starved.

It was 6:58. The clock ticked off the seconds.

"What can we do?" Mom asked.

The clock began sounding the Westminster Chimes, prologue for "top of the hour," followed by a slow counting: *Dong! Dong! Do . . .*

On the seventh "dong," all heard the rumbling, rolling, humming, grinding stops of a chain of cars, vans, and trucks.

"They're here! Let's greet them. Afterwards we'll carry breakfast out," Grandma said. Everyone in the kitchen stopped what they were doing and ran outside.

"Hello!"

"Hi!"

Hugs.

"Great to see you again!"

"You look younger every time we meet!"

Slaps on the back.

"Wow, these boys are growing fast."

"Like weeds!"

Laughs, shouts, shaking hands, hugs all around.

Then it was time for Max, Charles, Mom, Mrs. Ellen, and Grandma to begin carrying out goodies and placing them on the long tables. MFA members, having been raised to be gentlemen, pitched in. In ten minutes or less, tables were groaning under the weight of the breakfast feast.

When the beverage buffet was ready on the porch, Grandma announced, "Get your drinks. Please serve yourselves. Enjoy family-style platters, bowls, and baskets of goodies that you'll find filling every table, only inches from your plate. As you empty a bowl or platter, give a yell and refills will be delivered."

Max looked around. He saw tall, thin boys who were several years older than he. He saw a few women dressed in the finest fly-fishing uniform: khaki pants and shirts. He saw guys about Fred's age.

There were many older men, too, who'd been Grandpa's friends ever since they were boys. Among the older men Max spotted was environmental artist and storyteller Mr. Burt, who always insisted, "Just call me Burt." He was busy setting up an easel and placing his art pads on it, and beside it a little "milking stool" he liked to sit on. Cans of colored pencils, charcoal, and ink pens, a jar of water, a pallet, and tubes of watercolors were all waiting. Art materials were his stage, and with them he was a master entertainer.

Max looked around some more, but he didn't see Fred or the two new kids described as being close to his age. Had Charles fibbed? Max was ready to speak to his younger brother, possibly in a way that would get him in trouble, when just then, what did he see but Fred's fire-engine-red pickup truck zipping through the pasture from the house and parking behind the pony barn beside their mom's van.

As soon as Fred had cut the engine, doors began opening. Fred hopped out of the truck, followed by two kids with red, curly hair, wearing identical overalls and long-sleeved T-shirts. All three were laughing and chatting.

Max signaled Charles. "They're here," he mouthed.

Both boys ran to meet Fred and the new kids.

Even from a distance, Max felt good vibrations bouncing off these two new kids, who just happened to be twins.

Chapter 2

All Things Are Bright
and Beautiful

"Jamie and Joe, let me introduce you to my sons, Max and Charles," said Fred.

Inside, Max felt the special "happy warm" feeling he always felt when Fred introduced him and Charles as his sons. Not his "stepsons." His sons. It was only one word, but it was a big word that made a big difference to Max and Charles. It meant Fred was Dad no matter who their biological father had been. He divorced their mom when they were small and chose to never reenter their lives. He never offered gifts, never sent cards on birthdays or holidays.

Then Mom met Fred. They dated, got married, and then went to court, where Fred adopted them. The judge granted the request and no one ever contested it. Their big brother, Ralph, who was legally old enough to decide for himself, declared, "For sure, no matter what, this dude Fred is the man I call Dad."

"OK, you four, see ya' later. I'd better hurry and help your mom and grandmother with the breakfast stuff," Fred said. He waved as he dashed towards the kitchen. His job, doing whatever he was asked to do, had begun.

Fred's quick exit is his way of allowing us kids to get to know each other without any adults hovering around. Way cool, Max thought. Aloud, he asked the twins, "How do you know Fred?"

"He teaches at our school. It's the same school where our grandma teaches. I guess they work on some projects together," Joe said.

"Cool," said Charles.

Jamie and Joe were turning around and around, looking at the farmhouse, the yard, the woods, the pasture, and in the distance, the streams.

"You guys live here? Man, are you LUCKY," Joe said. He was the taller of the twins. His fuzzy red hair was shorter than Jamie's by about six inches.

"Yep, same farm and house our grandpa ALWAYS lived in. Well, ever since he was seven years old," Charles said. "How cool is that?"

The twins exchanged looks and smiled. Jamie, the shorter twin, said, "VERY cool. We live with our grandma in the house she grew up in. It isn't in the country. In fact, it's in Baltimore City. And it's not on a farm, but we do have a double-sized yard. We can take paths to the nearest stream and walk several blocks, and there's the park. We don't raise trout, but we do buy little fish for our aquarium ..."

"And a few bigger fish live outside in the pond Grandma made for us," added Joe.

Two boys? A boy and a girl? Max wasn't sure until he took a careful look at Jamie: hair longer, nose trimmer, eyes bigger, lips softer, eyebrows . . . plucked? OK, plucked eyebrows were the giveaway: Jamie was a girl. *Oh yeah! And she looks like the kind of girl who'll try to match any challenge her brother might try.* In some ways, she reminded Max of a girl he knew in Maine, the girl who'd been in his dream earlier that morning, before Charles woke him up: Zipper, from Deer Isle.

In the pause following their "home facts," Charles decided to change the subject. He pulled out his notepad and read off, "The schedule for today is . . ."

> *We greet.*
> *We eat.*
> *The trout tank truck arrives.*
> *Experts will organize.*
> *Fish scientists go to the trout pools*
> *where they net then carefully slip*
> *each brook into big, white, plastic buckets.*
> *A line of people form*
> *"the bucket brigade."*
> *It'll be person to person,*
> *one bucket following another*
> *down the line*
> *until each arrives*
> *beside the tank truck*
> *into the hands of expert fish biologists*
> *(the real trout pros)*

who count,
measure,
check each fish
for any illness they may have.
After each trout (hopefully)
passes a physical exam,
into the water-filled tank it goes.

"Sick fish? What kind of sick do you mean?" Joe asked.

"Well, I read a book, *Illnesses Fish Get*, part of an independent school project I did," Max answered. "According to some marine scientists, the big disease brook trout can get is a bacterial kidney disease."

"Man, that doesn't sound good," Joe said.

"Not good at all. Fortunately, they only rarely need operations to find out if the fish are healthy. No operations, no painkillers, no sewing them up afterwards. No, if a fish had to be cut open, it would be killed first and the tissue samples sent for study. As for the rest of the fish? Hopefully it would be used to feed other creatures. Usually marine biologists can tell if a trout is sick by watching them and examining their scales. They can tell a lot by watching their behavior."

"What do they look for?" Jamie asked.

"Well, how a fish swims, if the fish is not feeding well, if it's acting sort of lazy," Charles said.

"The fancy word for that is 'lethargic,'" Max added.

"Yeah, a word for a fifth-grade spelling test," Charles said. "They also check out brook trout reflexes and look for lesions, parasites, or any growths on the fish's skin or fins."

"Are these fish doctors doing *all* these tests, exams, on *each* trout today, right here?"

"Well, not all. I mean, for nine months, the trout have been here with Grandpa and members of MFA watching, looking for obvious stuff like not eating and acting lethargic. But individual examinations of their skin and fins are hard to do when they're all swimming around in the pools," said Charles.

"Exams are going to be done as each trout is taken from the net and placed into the truck's water tank?" Joe asked.

"These scientists are really sharp. They can tell quickly whether a fish is healthy or not. At least, I think so," Charles said.

Max said, "Charles is right. That's exactly what will happen, because they don't want any diseased fish placed into streams where wild fish are living."

"And you have lots of trout?" Jamie asked.

"This year, I think there are about 1,200-plus," Max answered.

"Whew! It is going to be a long day," Joe said.

"Well, for the fish scientists, yes, but Charles forgot to mention the environmental artist, Burt, who will be giving funny informative lectures as he sketches everything from doves and dogs to raccoons, buzzing insects, and tail-flipping fish. He's fun, a real pro."

"You know him . . . like, really well?" Joe asked.

"He's Grandpa's best friend," Charles said.

"Great!" said Jamie.

"Today Grandpa and some others will give

demonstrations and share tips on how to tie flies, for anyone interested," Max added.

"I want to learn to make my own. I'm really embarrassed when my fly gets caught in a tree and Grandma, or someone fishing near me, has to cut it down. I hate losing a fly anytime, but it's really bad when someone gave it to me as a gift. Or worse, they loaned it to me when we went fishing," Jamie said.

"You go fishing lots?" Max asked.

"Not lots. I like to fish when I get a chance. I love being out in nature. How about you?" Jamie asked.

"I love being in nature too. I fish, but I'm all thumbs when it comes to tying flies. I'm like you when I cast. Lots of times, my fly gets wrapped around a tree branch and I need help," Max said. "Maybe today, or some other time, I'll check out the fly-tying clinic. Where I definitely want to be is at our big pond when Grandpa and others are showing casting tips."

"BUT for now . . . BREAKFAST!" yelled Charles.

"Want to eat together, keep, uh . . . comparing our fishy hopes?" Jamie asked with a grin.

"Sure," Max said. *Oh boy*, he thought, *this is shaping up to be a good day.*

"Yeah," Jamie said.

"Last one to the breakfast table is a . . ." Charles yelled and took off.

"Rotten egg?" joked Joe.

"Yuck!" Two out of four groaned in chorus.

Max and Charles had never seen their grandparents' backyard filled with so many people. The quiet space between the tall oaks looked like a fairground. Men, women, a few girls, young adult men, and older teen guys gathered at the beverage buffet line. Chairs tilted, tops to table side, marked "place reserved," while fishing gear, caps, jackets, boots, shining metal rod cases, notebooks, and stacked boxes of fishing lures saved table places and seats.

Fortunately, besides the breakfast foods that Mom, Mrs. Ellen, and Grandma had prepared, people had brought extras. Most donations weren't as special as homemade cinnamon rolls and sticky buns. Some brought prepackaged foods from local shops and fast-food drive-thrus, but all snacks were accepted and appreciated. After all, it was the thought and the wish to contribute that counted the most.

People gathered to eat and filled platefuls with food. But as important as the big breakfast-brunch was, for most of the people there, it was a chance to enjoy time together—a reunion. The air hummed with conversation and anticipatory vibrations of the day's task. These trout-loving people shared their latest successes and failures in trying to lure wild brook trout with homemade flies and bugs. They swapped stories, and many shared groans, moans, and laughter as men, women, boys, and girls filled cups with coffee, tea, milk, or juice.

Following the line of adult leaders, Jamie, Joe, Charles, and Max got their drinks and found a table—sibling beside sibling, Joe and Jamie facing Max and Charles. They'd picked places at the end of a long table far away from a gathering of serious trout fly–tier competitors.

How did Max and Charles know where to sit? Which places would be near but out of ear range from serious fishermen, a place where they could talk "kid talk"? They'd first studied the group and seen fishermen hunched close to each other, sitting with little books on fishing by famous writers, like Reuben R. Cross, Art Flick, Nick Lyons, and Sparse Grey Hackle. Next to these plates were stacks of plastic fly boxes. In the spaces between plates, many had their log books held open with unused eating utensils. These serious fisherfolk held pencils capped with pink erasers in one hand while stabbing sausages and eggs with forks in the other. They took small bites and chewed their food on one side of their mouths, eating while causing as little interruption in their conversations as possible. Proper manners of talking while eating had been forgotten. They questioned each other on which fly worked best on last year's mayfly hatch and what materials were used to make it. Meanwhile, others discussed success using Quill Gordons, Hendrickson-Red Quill, Grey Fox, or Stonefly Creepers. It was a real Q and A breakfast.

"What stream were you on most days?"

"Morgan Run, Hunting Creek, and the Gunpowder."

"What months?"

"First of April, when slushy snow still crusted on the path and ice drops glistened like a curtain of diamonds hung over the bank all the way down until they touched the stream's surface. Sure is a pretty sight to see even when the fish aren't interested. I was there all of May and into June."

"Every day?"

"*Mostly. Lost a few when the weather was being too evil. Thunderstorms, hail as big as English walnuts . . . in the shell.*"

"*Best times?*"

"*Oh, I'm an early bird. I arrive before dawn. I like watching everything begin to awaken.*"

"*Are you there when sunrise begins to color the sky and the moon is still a beacon?*"

"*Yeah, I have a cabin I stay in, so midafternoon, when trout and most of nature are scarce to find, I take an afternoon snooze.*"

"*Me, I like fishing by moonlight best of all.*"

"*My favorite time is dusk.*"

"*Me too, fish at dusk as the air cools and after people who've been fishing all day go in for libations and dinners.*"

"*Yes, that would be me.*"

"*You're the guy who chooses night fishing? You have clamps attached to rubber wader feet, a cane support in one hand and your rod in the other?*"

"*Yep, that's me.*"

Voices hummed in tones several decibels below the high-pitched drone of the seventeen-year cicada songs.

"Do you really like to fish?" Max asked Jamie and Joe.

"I love science. For me, fly fishing is science," Joe said. "I get to study insects in spring and summer at all different times during the day. I also enjoy the math. You know, like how many feet should I make my back and forward casts? How far should I allow my dry fly to drift over stream or river calm pools or riffling ripples before I jerk my wrist to make my hook twitch in imitation of a real insect?"

"Yeah, taking what I've studied in a book and making

it real," Charles said in a dreamlike voice. Joe was speaking a language he understood. Charles was a real numbers sort of guy.

"Well, for me, it's really about going to a stream or river and just being," said Jamie. "I mean, don't get me wrong, I like trying to make something from feathers, fur, and artificial types of fuzz and threads come alive . . . sort of like a puppet, a marionette. But then, after a while, I just reel in my line, find a cozy notch, and sit. I watch the flying creatures, from insects to birds, and daydream about what it must be like to cruise on air. I always carry my drawing pad, ink pens, or charcoal pencils. And, well, I like to find words to describe what I'm seeing or feeling, or even maybe what the fish is feeling too. That's why I like this whole catch-and-release style of fishing."

"Well, I can relate," Max said. "I can't draw, but I do like to write."

"Really?" Jamie asked. "What kind of stuff do you write?"

"Uh, I keep a journal and—"

"Max writes really good poetry. In fact—"

"Charles!"

"In fact, he's published," Charles finished.

"Charles, I wish you'd learn to keep my secrets better," Max hissed.

"You write poetry? I think that's great!" Jamie said. "Don't you, Joey?"

"Yeah, I do," Joe said. "You see, our grandma is a published poet, and she teaches poetry. Jamie and I have had to learn lots of poems ever since we were really little."

"Cool!" Max and Charles said together. They grinned.

"We have this crazy thing of saying the same word at the same time," Max explained. "We're not twins. I'm three years older than Charles, but we were born at 10:00 p.m. on the same day of the same month."

"Crazy!" said Joe and Jamie together, and they laughed.

"We do it too, but then, we're twins."

"Ever hear a poem called 'The Fish'?" Max asked.

"By Elizabeth Bishop."

"Yes!"

"I love that poem. Talk about a true fishing reality check and one brave fish," said Jamie.

"And then the way it ends . . . 'rainbow, rainbow, rainbow'—"

"Yep, and then the narrator writes—"

"'And I let the fish go,'" Jamie said.

"Right. Just like catch and release."

"Great poem."

"Our grandpa read it to us lots when we were small. I think that poem is Grandpa's fly-fishing philosophy. Let the fish go," said Max.

"Makes sense," said Joe.

"Your grandmother is a poet and she taught you to write poetry for a long time?" Max asked.

Joe looked at Jamie. "Might as well clue them in," he said.

"OK. Well, you see, we only have our grandmother. Our grandfather and our parents were killed in an air crash when we were three years old. Grandpa was flying his little plane, a Cessna, and there was a bad storm . . ." Joe hesitated.

"We have some memories of them," Jamie added.

"And photographs Grandma shows us," Joe said. "She tells us many stories about them."

"It was hard for all three of us, but our grandmother was super strong, and she knew the arts can really help with grief, so she helped us to write. When we were really little, she was our 'scribe,' writing down our thoughts and feelings, before we could write," Jamie said.

"Then she has always cheered us on. She's always at every school event," Joe said.

"Always," added Jamie, thoughtfully.

Max and Charles were both very quiet as they listened to really tough stuff being told to them by two people they'd just met.

"Grandma used not just the arts but also sports, like fishing, to help us. And she found special camps for us to attend with other kids like us . . . well sort of. This year, we'll go to an Outward Bound camp in Maine for twelve- and thirteen-year-olds who have lost someone— or in our case, some*ones*—they love. I'll go canoeing, and Joe here will be—"

"On a weeklong kayaking-and-camping, island-to-island trip," Joe said.

"We can't wait. We've been to all kinds of support group–type programs, but the ones in Maine must be very cool."

"Very!" Max and Charles said together.

"We vacationed on Deer Isle in Maine for two weeks in 1985, and it was amazing!" Max exclaimed.

"Deer Isle?" Joe asked.

"An island just off the coast," Charles said.

"I know where it is. I've seen it on maps that were sent to Grandma. We'll be near it in Blue Hill, Brooklin, and Brooksville," Jamie said.

"And we're going back to Deer Isle again this summer," said Max. "At least that's the plan."

"Wow! That's great. I wonder if we'll all be up there at the same time," Joe said.

"Maybe Fred and your grandmother will know," said Max. Then he thought, *I wake up from a dream of Zipper, and now I meet the twins, who might meet Zipper too someday. How cool is that?*

Chapter 3

Beautiful Words, Wonderful Words, Wonderful Words Said to Wild Ones

Early Saturday morning, Grandpa fed the trout. He did it while everyone else was busy with breakfast preparations. This was his special time alone with his "brookies."

Twice a day for nine months, Grandma, Fred, Max, Charles, Mom, other family, friends, and designated members of the Maryland Fly Anglers had taken turns feeding these fish. But on this morning, Grandpa wanted to be the one, and only one, who fed them their last meal at the hatchery.

The brooks were three-inch fingerlings when they arrived in late September. Now, May 31, they'd grown much bigger. Now they were between fifteen and seventeen inches long. Over the months, Grandpa's trout had changed: little minnow-sized flickers had grown into real beauties. They were nearly twice as big as most wild brook trout and healthier than many raised in commercial hatcheries.

Many people, including Grandpa, considered wild brook trout the most beautiful of all trout and one of nature's loveliest works of art. Their bodies were covered in spots: light spots across a dark background, spots as squiggly as worms, and rose-colored side spots with blue halo-like circles. Their red and orange belly spots were as bright as sunsets. On top was a dorsal fin; near their bellies were lower fins, each with bright white stripes with black lines, as if someone had drawn them on with a Sharpie. They were sleek, graceful fish with few scales and no spines on their fins.

Early on this morning, Grandpa sat beside the hatchery pools and watched *Salvelinus fontinalis*, the Latin name for brook trout. "Little *fontinalis*," he whispered. "I must remember to tell Max and Charles your proper name. *Fontinalis* means 'from a fountain or a stream.' Indeed, you are fish who live only in the coldest, cleanest streams. I need to teach the boys your Latin name, even though, to me, you'll always be brookies."

As Grandpa fed his babies, he lectured them on the dangers of living in the wild. He wished each a long and happy life. By afternoon these fish all would be relocated, freed into their real wilderness habitat. Yes, free, but no longer protected by concrete hatchery walls. Free was frightening. Their new home wouldn't be in someone's aquarium. It would be in Hunting Creek, located in Maryland's Catoctin Mountains, where they'd be "fished for fun" with barbless hooks. If a fish should be critically hurt, if it swallowed a hook and appeared to be suffering, fishing folk were advised to kill the fish and then leave it on the river bank as food for other wild creatures.

Brook trout are Maryland's only native trout. In the 1970s, fishermen and wildlife naturalists noticed there were fewer and fewer of them in streams, and in recent years the population had steadily decreased. Environmentalists and fly fishers who loved the challenges of catching these frisky fish were worried. Runoff water from town buildings, housing developments, and farms were often filled with dreaded fertilizers and killer insecticides. Many wild creatures were being killed as development increased; some had become extinct.

Grandpa and others would not sit quietly and let this happen. In the mid-1970s, he and friends convinced members of the Maryland Fly Anglers, or MFA, that The Property's stream conditions made for an excellent trout hatchery. Grandpa told them that for years, he'd studied streams where brook trout thrived, and studied waters ever since he was a little boy fishing with a string and a pole. The stream running down from the Big Spring on The Property was clear and clean, with brown, pink, and white quartz pebbles lining its bottom. He told people, "This spring-fed stream is the perfect habitat for raising tiny brook fingerlings into healthy fish."

He convinced wildlife organizations in the state, and during the summer of 1978, the hatchery was built. It was designed with Grandpa's knowledge: two long, deep, cement-sided pools with natural sand and pebbly bottoms, partially shaded by shrubs, evergreens, and hardwood trees. It was not the usual fish farm. Grandpa's trout were not babied, and though they were fed Purina Trout Chow twice a day, they also ate naturally: vegetation growing nearby or falling over the tiny dams and drifting from the Big Spring onto Pool #1 and Pool #2.

Along with the chow, the trout fed on insects that fell into the pools, and even an occasional frog or claw-snapping crayfish. Then the MFA built removable screens (wooden frames that looked like big doors covered with chicken wire) to keep the trout pools safe from the most dangerous enemies: great blue herons, raccoons, and other larger predators.

Always the brook trout arrived in the fall and were raised through winter into spring. Grandpa called his trout hatchery a "tough-love boot camp for future trout," believing they were well prepped for the harsh reality of future lives in mountain streams.

While the breakfast feast was being prepared, Grandpa whispered words of wisdom to the brook trout, praying in his own words a prayer based on those said by ancient Native American spirit guides, his wishes for his little brood of brookies.

May you always find safe homes in deep pools.
Should you be caught by clever fly fishers,
may barbless hooks only catch in your lip
and never be swallowed.
May you enjoy years flashing your colorful fins,
delighting all lucky enough to enjoy seeing you
as you battle: matching wits with your feistiness.

May each of you be let free again,
to swim in your shadowy, hidden worlds
and there may you reside, living many years,
becoming wisdom keepers of your own kingdoms.

Chapter 4

And They Waded in the Waters

"Where are they?" Charles asked, looking at his watch.

"Who?"

"The official Marine Fisheries scientists and their big fish tank trucks."

"When are they supposed to arrive?" Joe asked. He chased slippery-thin slices of sugary fresh strawberries around and around his paper plate with a plastic fork.

"8:30," Max said. "What time is it, Charles?"

"8:28."

"Well, give them two more minutes before you start complaining," Jamie said with a grin.

Hmm, thought Max, *she's only known Charles a little over an hour and already figured out some of his time quirks, AND she responds to his time manic-ness in a right-on way. Yeah.*

"8:29," Charles announced.

"Listen! I think I hear loud motors coming in this direction," Joe said. He stabbed the strawberry slices with his fork, opened his mouth, and sucked them in. "Yum!"

They stopped talking and chewing, and listened.

Yes, they heard the sound of big trucks gearing down, brakes squeaking, and then gravel crunching, growing louder as big trucks twisted and turned up the driveway.

Exactly at 8:30, two fish tank trucks parked between the house and the garage. Doors opened and people got out.

"Perfect!" said Max.

"Precisely. Right on the second. Perfection," Jamie said.

All MFA club members and others, including Max, Charles, Jamie, and Joe, scooped down the last of breakfast. They gathered plates, spoons, knives, forks, and paper napkins, and cleaned their table places. They threw away trash and placed reusables into sudsy water. When they were done, they gathered near the state Freshwater Fisheries Program men and women to receive instructions.

Many clean white buckets were distributed. A human chain from truck to trout pools was formed. The "Net Man" was the first dipper. He was the master at this task. He went to the lower pool, the one closest to the house, wearing rubber waders that went to his chest. But he didn't step into the crowded trout pool; he'd do that later, when it was less fish-filled. Instead, he bent over and dipped a long, wood-handled net into the seething hatchery water. Slowly he lifted the woven-cotton string net. All standing near saw he'd captured three flopping trout. He quickly lowered them into a white bucket, which was half-filled with water from the spring.

The morning's work had officially begun.

Net Man dipped again while someone placed another half-filled bucket next to him. Ten identical white buckets waited, ready to be filled and then passed. The Net Man continued to dip and fill, and always the next person in line took the bucket and passed it to another and then another. Bucket after bucket of wiggling trout were carefully passed, moment by moment, hour by hour.

To prevent trout from splashing, bruising, or flopping out onto the ground, buckets were passed as slowly as possible from man to man to woman to woman to teenagers to children, all ages, mixed together, young to old.

Finally, each bucket arrived into the hands of qualified marine biologists, who weighed, measured, and checked the health of each trout before lifting it to the top of the truck, where another marine biologist, Merry Anne, swished the fish into the tank truck.

After about an hour and a half, Merry Anne called down. "Who's the group leader or leaders raising these trout?"

"Over there!" Max heard someone from MFA shout. They were pointing at Grandpa and several of his pals.

"I need to speak to them later. Tell them not to dare go away," Merry Anne said.

I wonder if Grandpa and MFA are in trouble, Max thought. *I'm going to hang close by and see what this official has to say.*

Five minutes later (as Charles clocked it and told Max later), Merry Anne asked for a pause in the action. She put down her bucket and other equipment, took off her rubber gloves, and then nimbly climbed the ladder rungs from the top of the truck to the ground. A final leap and she had landed on the grassy side lawn. Within minutes, Max saw her by Grandpa's side.

Max crept closer to hear what she was going to say, but he could have stayed where he was.

"Can everyone just stop for a moment? Catch a breath. Rest," Merry Anne said in a very loud, commanding voice.

Everyone heard and stopped. They froze, like freeze tag, in whatever position they'd been in.

Seeing everyone as still as statues and in a variety of work positions, Max thought of the fairy tale where characters were "frozen" until the spell was magically broken.

"I wanted all of you to know I visit many hatcheries. My work, and actually my pleasure, takes me to wilderness streams where catch-and-release rules are enforced and where I make studies of many kinds of fish, especially brook trout. I know this is the only private hatchery in the State of Maryland where brook trout are being raised, and I must tell you, I am amazed." She paused and put her hand on Grandpa's shoulder.

"Well, we love our brookies," Grandpa said.

"When I return to my office on Monday, I write my report to the Freshwater Fisheries Program, and I'll be sure to describe this great little hatchery, and the amazing

volunteers, who are raising these healthy brook trout."
She shook Grandpa's hand.

"Others should be recognized too. MFA Club members here today, where are you all?" Grandpa said.

"Yes, raise your hands," said Merry Anne.

Max looked around and saw MFA members reluctantly raising their hands. They were a shy group. He heard Burt "ahem" by his side, and before he could look, Burt had pushed up Max's hand. Nearby he saw others push up Charles's, Mom's, and Grandma's hands as well.

"Goodness, what a large group of supporters!"

"And some are missing," Grandpa said. "Where's that Fred? I know he's here somewhere."

"I'll grab him," Grandma said, popping back into the kitchen, where Fred was preparing things for lunch. "Here he is!" Grandma said, pushing Fred out onto the cement porch. "Fred and his friend Pat, who couldn't make it here today, both helped our grandsons, Max and Charles, scare away a great blue heron who was after our trout at sunset one May night."

"I applaud you all," Merry Anne said. "And a special round of applause for the family who keep this hatchery on their lovely farm."

Everyone applauded the family.

Grandpa looked like he wished he could sneak away, but Burt, standing beside him, put his arm around Grandpa's shoulders.

The marine biologist who had been dipping the fish from the pool came forward.

"Hey, everybody, I'm applauding the family too! And

I have an announcement. No more trout are in Pool #1. It is also 11:00 a.m., and if the cooks are ready, I think it's probably a good time to take a lunch break. We'll begin Pool #2 at . . ." He looked at Grandma and Fred.

"Lunch will be ready in ten minutes or so," Grandma said.

"Then we'll begin on Pool #2 at 12:30," the biologist announced.

There was a cheer.

Max knew he'd be needed to help serve lunch. He looked around for Charles and found him talking with Jamie and Joe. *OK, maybe they'd like to help too,* Max thought.

"Hey! Charles!" Max shouted as he walked towards them.

"Hey, Max! We're telling Charles we'd like to help," said Joe.

"Yep, we've had lots of practice bussing tables," Jamie said.

"Perfect," said Max.

"Ex-cell-ent," added Charles.

Chapter 5

Respecting Creatures Large and Small

After a lunch of grilled hot dogs and burgers, salads, chips, and melons chilled overnight in the cold spring waters and sliced into triangles (portable and easy nibbling), and after fisherfolk, on pause from work, had discussed best techniques, rods, lines, reels, sinkers, and flies (wet and dry), lunch ended. The time had arrived to re-form the human chain of bucket passers. All went to their assigned places: buckets or kitchen crew.

But before they had even reached the back porch, Fred made an announcement: "Our youngest workers have worked hard today. We appreciate all they've done. To show our appreciation best, our legendary artist/storyteller Burt will now reward them with some stories and drawings."

"Ah, man, I wish I was thirteen again," moaned

Madison, a forty-something member of the MFA.

"Madison, dear lad," Burt said, "in comparison to my age, you *could* be thirteen. Now, tell you what, work hard like the fine young man I know you are and I'll make it up to you . . ." He paused, surveying the group. "And to other catchers and fly-tying fisherfolk here, I'll be telling a big whopper fish tale, filled with charcoal illustrations, at the next MFA evening during the after-hours meeting."

Applause. Laughter. Cheers.

"After we finish KP duty, we're invited to go join Burt," Charles said.

"We're almost done," said Max, swabbing down the surface of a long table. "Two more tables to wipe and then I'm done."

"I'm on my last one," said Joe.

"Two more for me too," Jamie said. "How about you, Charles?"

"One and a half." He looked at his watch. "Be done in two minutes." He was wiping his tables in swirls and dashes. Max, Joe, and Jamie were surprised when they saw how Charles's tables sparkled when he was done in exactly 120 seconds. The secret known by Charles but not revealed to the others was that these two tables had not been used.

The three thirteen-year-olds and one ten-year-old washed up in a rubber tub set out for just that purpose. They checked in with Grandma, Mom, and Mrs. Ellen, who gave their approval. Ten minutes later, Jamie, Joe, Charles, and Max stood in front of Burt and his easel.

Burt was bent over and rooting through a cardboard box of colored pencils. He placed each "pick" in the front pocket of his fly-fishing vest. Then he took from an old tin can a fat, messy charcoal chunk. Slowly he straightened, stretched his back, and looked at the row of four standing-like-statues kids. He winked and then looked away, continuing to organize his drawing materials, placing each where he wanted it, with a grip on the piece of charcoal. He adjusted his worn, tan, floppy cloth hat so it sat higher above his shaggy eyebrows, pushed his eyeglasses down on his nose, and coughed once. In a quiet voice, which sounded more like the raspy call of a wild fox than a grandfatherly man, he said, "What do we have here? A standing ovation before the show begins? Now that intimidates even an old 'grizzly' like me. Go get yourselves chairs to sit on. Then I'll begin."

Four flashes found four folding chairs and, following in single file, returned in less than four minutes, in less time, in fact, than it takes to reread this sentence.

Burt pointed out places for chairs, and when done, there was a semicircle about four feet away from where he stood. "Fine. Fine. Fine. Fine!" He said as each chair was positioned and each young person sat.

"Now," Burt said, "first." He rubbed his bristling chin with the knuckle of the hand that held the charcoal. "I have a question? How does one begin?"

"Uh," Max looked at Jamie, who looked at Joe, who looked at Charles, who looked at Max.

"Yes?" Burt asked.

"Uh," Max suggested, "At the beginning?"

"Hmm," Burt seemed to ponder this answer for a whole ten seconds. "Very true, good, but to be more specific, as an artist, or so they say I am, as an artist and someone known to tell a yarn, one begins with a first line."

Burt took a black drawing pencil and drew a two-inch line, paused, and extended it into a wide circle. "Now, my young friends, you have the beginning. But before we continue, I'll need to be introduced to two of you?"

"Oh, sorry. Burt, this is Jamie and her twin brother, Joe. Their grandmother works at the same school as Fred," said Max.

"I'm three minutes older," Joe said.

Jamie wrinkled her nose and squinted her eyes. She turned to Burt. "But I started talking first." She looked back at Joe and whispered, "So there!"

"And have not stopped talking since," Joe said. He grinned at Jamie.

Jamie grinned back at Joe.

"Inside joke," Joe announced.

Burt's eyes sparkled at this answer.

"Jamie and Joe, do you live near here?"

"No, we live with our grandmother in Roland Park," Joe said.

"Oh yes, Roland Park," said Burt. "I know it well."

"It's a neat place to live. Not as great as this," Joe said, looking around, "but considering it's in the city, it's OK, and there're lots of streams and old trees."

"*And* this summer, a chorus of cicadas songs," added Jamie.

"I'm sure. All those old trees and Victorian homes built on double lots, surrounded by parks, and basically wild wooded areas, untouched for many years—that creates delightful sanctuaries for cicadas. This summer, the seventeen-year cicadas emerging from their under-world homes must be singing their little hearts out," Burt said. He returned to his drawing pad, made a few quick strokes with a thinner black pencil. When he stopped, they saw it was a cicada flying over the circle.

"The shadow of this big bug might pique some interest from critters living below," Burt said.

He lightly brushed the chunk of charcoal across the paper and then used his fingertips to smudge a flying-cicada shape inside the circle.

"Then if that someone resting below is interested, they just might 'dimple' the surface calm. This would be especially noticed when water of a deep pool is smooth . . . as smooth as . . . well, they often say 'smooth as glass.' Of course, glass is hard and shatters. So that's not the right simile to use. A new simile is needed." He shifted the charcoal into his other hand and, with a drawing pencil, made a dot just under the cicada.

"How about smooth as silence?" Jamie asked.

"Good one. Poetic. I like that," Burt said with a grin. "But now, who might the dimple maker be?"

"A curious fish?" Joe suggested.

"Let's see." Burt began drawing. This time, he used different-colored pencils, sketching a long shape at the bottom of the first circle he'd drawn.

The four young people watched a fish appear.

It's as if his drawing pencils are cutting open a paper-covered container and he's freeing what's been hidden inside, Max thought. Then as Burt added color dots, he revised his idea: *Or maybe what's being released was eased free from a trap to become life on paper.*

"It's a brook trout!" Jamie said.

"And how do you know that?" Burt asked. He continued coloring spots but looked at his audience.

"Well, the colors look right, and also the dot patterns. I'll know for sure when you add the fins," Jamie said.

"*IF* I add fins . . . I may not . . . no, I will," said Burt. He laughed his gruff little laugh. His laugh sounded like someone clearing their throat, ending in a "hee-hee" or "haw-haw."

Taking orange, black, and white colored pencils, Burt added the fins. The white and sharp black lines were the details Jamie was looking for.

"See! White and black, that makes it a brook trout for sure," she said. "No other trout has fins with those markings."

"This girl knows her trout," Burt said. He stopped drawing for a moment to look at Jamie. He tapped the brim of his hat, saluting her. Then he said to the boys, "Very impressive." He returned to the drawing. "Of course, this brook trout isn't really interested in eating a cicada . . . I don't think. It's May and there's a delicious nymph a trout can't resist, flying between the cicada and the dimpled water."

As they watched, Burt drew a tiny little insect carrying a cluster of yellow. "This little insect needs to drop her eggs, but . . . I'm not sure the trout will let her. Unless, of course, there's a bigger distraction to take a trout's mind off yummy nibbles."

Burt stuck the smaller colored pencils into his pocket and, from the can, took out five thicker pencils: dark green, pale green, yellow, white-white, and black. He began to draw tall stalks. "Later in the summer, these will have big brown heads and will be called ..."

"Cattails?" asked Max.

"Cattails, right you are!" said Burt. He took a thinner green pencil and drew lines from the top of the paper down to touch the circle. Others hung down. "And this might be?" he asked.

"Grass and weeds?" suggested Charles.

"Yes, indeed, I think that's what they are. Now, someone else needs to appear. Someone who'll keep Mr. or Ms. Brook Trout hiding down in the shadows." Burt worked with thick black pencils, and within seconds appeared ...

"A raccoon!" all four said together.

"That's right. Perhaps fishing for trout or maybe ..." Burt began drawing with colored pencils again: circles and more circles. Soon the four watchers recognized lily pads—white and yellow shapes, blooming white lilies with yellow centers. Then with green, white, and brown, and a few little red lines, Burt had drawn a frog sitting on a lily pad close to the raccoon. The pad and frog were sleepily drifting over the back of the brook trout.

"And there's a story with several endings," Burt said. He signed his name, tore the paper from the pad, and let it fall onto the grass beside the easel.

"Could a story like that really happen?" Charles asked.

"Ah, well, you know there's really only one way to find out," Burt said. "You must enter places where nature blooms." He drew as he described how to enter nature. Each sentence became a new illustration on another piece of art paper, colorful, big drawings similar to ones seen in some art galleries.

"You must go and listen." Burt made a drawing of circles. He tore the paper off and dropped it.

"Go and watch," he said, making many eyes in all colors and sizes. He tore off the paper and let it fall, landing beside the others.

"Go and feel the wind," he said, drawing clouds, leaves, grasses, and balloons.

"Go and know the flow of all the many waters you can discover." Burt drew a spring, a stream, a river, an ocean, a waterfall, a lake, and a pond. Again he tore away the paper and dropped it.

"You must go and allow yourself to be. It may take time. It may take many visits to many places over many years. Or it may happen all at once, right away, and then go away and not happen again for a long time. But if you are patient and if you open yourself up, I know it'll happen to each of you. And you'll always be something more because of it. You'll have become someone who knows the power of nature."

Burt had drawn a picture of all four of the young people who were watching him draw. "See, this is you, all four of you, finding what nature will want to give you." He tore off the piece of paper and handed it to them.

Then he drew four more pictures, an individual portrait for each.

He stopped drawing and turned to look at his audience.

"Now then, there is a pond waiting for you, a field pond in an old apple orchard. I know Max and Charles go there all the time. This is where you need to go now on a search for what I've just been talking about. I'll take these drawings back to the house and give them to your grandmother, Max and Charles. She'll put them someplace safe in case you want them. If not, let me know. I'll give them to someone else."

"We want them!"

"For sure!"

"So cool you made them for us!"

"Thanks, Burt."

"Yeah, thanks!"

"Thanks so much."

"Thank you!"

"And thank you," Burt said, tapping the brim of his old worn hat. "One more thing I want you to nestle and store in your gray matter. Each person needs to seek and find their place of contemplation. In quiet places, we discover portals that lead us on a step-by-step journey, which helps us learn more about who we are. Here's a hint. Each of you is as different as the four elements—earth, wind, water, and fire. Each of you will discover a portal into *your* own place in nature. Growth begins once you find which element you are, when you enter places where that element is primary."

The wizardly fly fisher, artist, storyteller, and wise man stopped talking. He turned away and began gathering his art supplies. Then he headed back to the place where the fly tiers were gathering. As he passed each of the four young people who had been his captive audience for an hour, he placed a rough, gnarled hand on their shoulder in a "good luck" gesture. As he did, each thanked him once again.

They waited motionless in silence until Burt had joined the fly-tying group.

Chapter 6

"Still, Still, Still"

"The pasture pond is over here," Max said. "Follow us."

Charles led the way, walking from the yard to the parking area, passing barns, chicken coops, and barrels filled with feed sacks and many brimming with water buckets. Then to the worn, silver-gray, wooden rail fence, which he climbed as he had ever since he was five years old—up, swing legs over, down, then a leap, landing in the soft, thick, unmown pasture grasses. As soon as he landed, he began running.

Max and the others followed: walking, climbing, leaping, landing, and running through silky grasses and weeds. No worry about rambunctious rams, nippy ponies, territorial roosters, or disagreeable geese. The farm animals were gated inside their coops, paddocks, and barns in preparation for later, when fly fishermen and fisherwomen would practice casting lines with barbless hooks into hula hoops big and small. Later they'd cast into the pond.

But casting practice wouldn't begin until all hatchery trout were caught and driven away in the tank trucks, and the hatchery pools were drained and made ready to be raked clean. The rest of spring and summer, Grandpa's pools would be empty of trout but partially filled with water, making them a welcoming home for all wild creatures that thrive in clean, spring-fed streams.

The four arrived at the farm pond one at a time. They chose their own places. Each stood alone. They followed Burt's directions to look for their own "portal," which would lead each to discover more about who they were, what places in nature they matched, and maybe even who they would BE someday.

There was no wind. The water appeared flat, quiet. Tall reeds growing along the shore were still. Everything seemed motionless.

After finding their place, each sat. Each stared into the calm water and waited.

What will happen? What will we see? Max wondered.

Would they all see something, or would the mystery of water be revealed to only one? Who would relate best to water and possibly find their portal there?

What was Burt talking about? Max thought. *And what is a portal anyway? What could happen? Would each person change, or not, once they found their matching element?* He kept focused on the calm water. *Mom would call this meditation.*

As Max watched, he saw the pond surface was not still at all but filled with action. Tiny insects with blue, silver, and gold, clear as tissue, batted their wings as they flew above it. *Mayflies?* Max wondered. He'd seen pictures of them in Grandpa's fish books. He knew it was the time of the year when these tiny insects were charmed by quiet, ruffling water. Some of them were dabbing yellow eggs in places where hopefully they would be safe, and the cycle of egg to nymph to mayfly would continue over the next year. *But mayflies and their eggs are tasty delights to many fish, particularly wise old trout,* he thought.

Max saw fish making dimples. *Just like in Burt's drawing . . . dimples on the silky-smooth surface, noses pushing up, eyes looking to see what was flying above.* All stayed calm. No splashes.

Max saw more. He saw water spiders (some call them water skaters) go skimming by. Then when he shifted his position, he startled a frog. It leaped from bank to pond, rippling the calm.

I remember swimming in the Lily Pond on Deer Isle. I remember when I floated on my back, I began to feel like I was one with water. I wonder, Max thought. And then he knew—though he was not the competitive swimmer Charles was—water was where he felt most part of nature. *Water must be my portal into the world of nature,* Max thought, and then knew, it was.

I've always liked all kinds of water: springs, streams, rivers, ponds, lakes, and bays, and the great roaring rhythms of ocean waves. When I'm near a water place, I'm the happiest. Each time I must leave it, I keep looking back, making secret promises to myself—and it—that I'll return soon. I guess I'm like a fish, like a brook trout. Water is my element.

Max sighed. He felt content watching the living water in front of him. It was quiet, peaceful, still . . . still . . . still . . . still . . . until.

Chapter 7

Close Encounters with Wild Ones

"Have we been here long enough? I mean really, Max, there are other places to show our guests."

Max looked up. Charles, who was actually eight inches shorter than Max, towered over him, a shadow blocking the bright afternoon sunlight.

"Uh, sure, I guess, if that's what you think is best? What about what Burt suggested we do?" Max mumbled. He was having trouble leaving the calm place he'd begun to slide into. *Water, my portal,* he thought.

"I'm content to stay here," Jamie said.

She was sitting down in the long grass a few feet from Max. "I like being here by the pond. I've been watching tiny flickers flying. Now look, Charles, you're movement is making a breeze brush through the cattail reeds. See? Those old, brown tops have not completely fuzzed out.

Oh, there go bits of it now, off into the wind. See? It looks like a ball of tiny, white cotton threads or a piece of free-flying fluff. The old leaves are dark green, bent, and broken. They hardly move at all. A few inches above the tallest grass, new pale-green leaves and stalks have begun to grow. And over there," she pointed at the giant willow.

A few clouds and now a slight breeze had begun.

"There's wind now, see?" Jamie continued. "And over there, by the stream, that big willow has new leaves. See how the wind is making those long boughs lift." She was silent for a few moments and then added, "I guess I know what it is I'm drawn to. It's wind. It's air. I've always loved hearing the wind. Have you guys ever heard the song about the wind's name? Mariah. I wish my mom had given me that name. Maybe when I'm older, I'll change my name to it. You know, many nights I've dreamed I was like a giant bird, flying." Jamie said.

"Yeah, and a big bird you'd be, but a brainy one," Charles said. He acted bored with all her wordy description. "OK, Max connects with water. Jamie connects with air. What about you, Joe?" Charles asked.

"I don't know yet. I want to go over there. See? See where those older trees are growing at the edge of the woods line? There's something over there I want to see," Joe said.

"OK," said Charles. He looked at his watch. "I think we have time to explore this element/portal thing some more. I've an idea, but I need to go up into our tree house to think."

"Good idea," Max said.

"I'll check back with you all in about thirty minutes," Charles said.

"Me too," said Joe.

Both Joe and Charles left, leaving Jamie and Max pondside.

"There are so many insects flying here," Jamie said. "I watch them and, too, the clouds. See, Max, see how soft and white, and how quickly they go feathering by us?" She was on her back, looking straight up.

Max tilted his head. He looked above the pond to the blue sky and the clouds Jamie had described. "Yep, nice," he said. Then he looked back at the pond's surface. It was like a mirror, and in it he saw the sky and cloud reflections. "Hey, Jamie, I can look at the top of the pond and see your world of sky and clouds . . . I can see them while looking at my favorite nature element."

"Cool," Jamie said.

Then Max saw something skittering on top of the water. It was all legs and was making a splashy mist. This was not the kind of wake a water spider (skater) made. It was not the dabbing of an insect or the fluffy landing of a bird's feather. It certainly wasn't the "bloopy" splash of a frog. Max leaned in as close to the pond as he dared, not wishing to frighten it, and then he laughed.

"What are you laughing at?" Jamie asked, turning to look his way.

"I'm watching the most awkward swimmer I've ever seen. Look! It's a spider."

"Where?"

"There."

"Wow, how funny." Jamie began to laugh.

The spider's long legs were making stitchery-twitchy movements as it went from a rock by the reeds to another rock farther away on the shore bank.

"Have you ever seen a spider go across the water like that?" Jamie asked Max.

"Never. It's a first for me," Max said.

A few minutes went by, and then Jamie turned to Max. "When I go home, I'll have to write about this spider in a book Joe and I are making with my grandmother."

"You're writing a book?"

"Well, actually, we're writing a couple of books. We've both been writing for a long time. Ever since . . . ever since the plane went down and our granddaddy, Mom, and Daddy died. One is a book about memories, and the other . . ." Jamie stopped.

"Yes?"

"I'm hoping you don't think this is silly or dumb or too sad or . . ." Jamie said.

"I know about sad too," Max said.

"You do?"

"Yes. Not like you, but like being a family that's different. It's because my bio dad didn't want to stay married to my mom anymore. So when I was four and Charles was one, he left and we've never seen him since."

"And Fred is?"

"He's our stepdad, but we don't use the word 'step.' He is our real dad as far as we're concerned. Even our older brother, Ralph, thinks of Fred as Dad."

"Great you have Fred and your mom," Jamie said.

"It's great you have your grandmother, right?"

"Oh yeah, she's fun and really young-acting. I guess maybe it's because she's a teacher and has to stay up on how to talk with kids and know stuff they like and stuff they find stupid."

"Yeah, it helps when the adults in your life still GET what it means to be a kid." Max looked back at the pond and added, "I write all the time. And someday . . . well, someday I hope to be a writer, but promise you won't tell."

"Cross my heart and toes, and promise to eat raw skunk-cabbage leaves, should I slip up. But Max, since Joe and I write, it's no big deal. What kind of stuff do you write?"

Yeah, here comes the big deal, thought Max, *the possible giant turnoff, but OK, I'll be honest.*

"Well, like Charles already told you, I write poetry and I keep a journal," Max said. "And I even write stories."

"Cool," Jamie said. Her face was one big smile.

"Really? You don't think it makes me sound like some nerd?"

"Nah, 'cause some of the greatest poems are tough stuff I've seen guys write and not some sappy, sugary, yucky, kissy-poo crap too many girls my age are writing," Jamie said with a cringe.

"Hey, you know that poem, a sonnet, Shakespeare wrote where he describes a woman but not in a sick-sweet way?"

"You mean the one that begins, *'My mistress' eyes are nothing like the sun,'* right?" Jamie asked.

"That's it. Can you recite it?" Max said, turning to face her. He sat up as tall as he could sit.

"Sure. Can you?" Jamie rolled over and sat up also.

They sat cross-legged on the grassy pond bank.

"I think so. Shall we try? You just gave the first line. Now I need to come up with the second. The challenge will be for both of us to recite every other line," Max said. *Jeez*, he thought, *I'm glad Mom just taught me this poem.*

"Let's do it. AND it's your turn," Jamie challenged.

"OK, next line is, *'Coral is far more red than her lips' red.'* Notice he just repeated 'red' two times in a row. That's a poetic no-no," said Max.

"Hmm, you'd think ol' Will would have known better. Next line is, *'If snow be white, why then her breasts are dun.'* Pretty racy stuff."

Blush, thought Max. *Ugh, just play it cool, man.*

"Yep, a censored version might be 'her chest is dun,'" he said. Next line is, *'If hairs be wires, black wires grow on her head.'* Not exactly soft to touch."

"No, let's see, oh yeah, right . . . *'I have seen roses damask'd, red and white.'* I think he was having trouble fitting what he wanted to say in iambic pentameter," Jamie laughed.

"Da-daah, da-daah, da-daah, da-daah, da-daah . . ."

"Da-daah, da-daah, da-daah, da-daah, da-daah!" finished Jamie.

"Ten short-long syllables per line are tricky to write. Sonnets aren't easy, though this is number 130 out of the 145 that we know Shakespeare wrote," Max said.

"Are you stalling?" Jamie asked.

"No, I know what comes next. *'But no such roses see I in her cheeks,'* right?"

"Yep. OK, here come my two favorite lines. *'And in some perfumes is there more delight.'*"

"Ha-ha-ha," Max laughed. "*'Than in the breath that from my mistress reeks.'* Bet she loved reading that!"

"But most likely very true. Next, *'I love to hear her speak, yet well I know.'* Ready?"

"Sure. *'That music hath a far more pleasing sound.'* Wonder if he'd say the same if he heard some of the rock bands playing around these days?" Max grinned.

"He might have wanted to revise his line. OK then, *'I grant I never saw a goddess go.'* I imagine goddesses must have stepped lightly or only flown around back then."

"Yep. *'My mistress, when she walks, treads on the ground.'* And we are near the very end," Max said.

"You know this sonnet really well."

"So do you."

"Shall we say the final couplet in unison?" Jamie asked.

"Why not."

And together they recited the end of Shakespeare's Sonnet 130:

> *And yet, by heaven, I think my love as rare*
> *As any she belied with false compare.*

They applauded themselves and yelled, "Bravo! Bravo!"

"A poem in which the great Bard was making fun of silly similes that were used to describe people," Jamie said.

"Yes, this is a poem my mom uses when she's teaching older kids how to write when they describe people, places, and things the way they really are and not by using, as you said, silly similes, which are all fluff," Max said.

"How does she get around the 'breast' word?" Jamie asked. "Just curious."

"I think Mom changes it to 'chest' when teaching a really immature group. But I think, with more mature kids, she just plunges in, after an introduction explaining Shakespeare more."

"OK, let's have a language duel. Who can think up the most disgustingly sugary poetic rhymed couplets," Jamie suggested.

"The gauntlet has been tossed," Max laughed. He pulled up and threw some weeds into the air. On the mild wind, they scattered closer to Jamie than to him. "And it is decided, you begin."

"Hmm," Jamie responded. Then she said,

Oh sweet fluffy flower
I love to smell your cool flavor.

"You never said it couldn't be slant rhyme. You?" Max was ready:

Lovely dude-ette, you're so rad,
your smile makes me feel glad.

"Dude-ette and rad?"

"I was using current slang. We never said that would be bad."

"True. Fun. Here's more slang."

You are bogus to the max!
You're a wiggin' ax attack.

She laughed and so did Max. Then Max said,

Ah, very fresh and cool
we have tied this duel.

"The end."

"The end."

"The end of what?" asked Joe as he strolled back from the woods.

"Dueling wordplay," Jamie said. "You know, like what WE do on long car rides with Grandma."

"Got it." Joe sat down between Max and Jamie.

"Did you find the element you feel is your portal?" Jamie asked.

"I think so. Not quite sure. Not ready to commit yet. Where's Charles?" Joe asked.

"Still up in our tree fort, I guess," Max said. "Shall we go over there? You haven't seen it yet."

"Think he'll be gnarly about it?" Jamie asked, using another eighties slang word.

"Doubt it. He thinks our tree fort is 'choice,' as they say," said Max.

"Dude," laughed Joe.

The tree fort had been built in a large winesap apple tree on the other side of the pond. Many years ago, there had been an orchard, but now only a few trees remained. Fred and Pat helped Ralph, Max, and Charles build the fort as a place the boys could consider their own space.

"It's over there," Max said as they approached it. "Let me go first and see if Charles is there."

"Sure," Joe and Jamie said together.

Max crept up to the old tree and climbed ladder boards nailed into its trunk. He slipped his head through a square cut in the main platform and looked. Then he quietly backed down the ladder and ran back to Jamie and Joe.

"He's there napping, the rascal. He always gets me up at first light, loves to nap in warm sunny spots, and never wants to miss a sunset, and when the stars are bright or the moon is full, he's ready to be outside again," Max reported to the others.

"Wonder if he likes being followed by moon shadows. I love full-moon shadows, but it's hard to find them where we live. I bet you can see them really well here," Joe said.

"Oh, yes. On a super-black night, the full moon is bright and tree limbs look like parallel beams to balance on. Then in winter, when the moon is full, it's brightest on new snow, but brrr, cold," Max said. "We have some stars, but the best stars we ever saw were in Maine, August 12, almost two years ago. It was like they were falling right on top of us."

"Oh, we understand, right, Joe? We saw stars like that one summer when we were staying at the ocean. It felt like they were going to shower down upon us. It was beautiful, and scary too."

"Got you," said Max.

"So what should we do about Charles? Leave him sleeping or . . ." Joe said. He stopped.

They heard voices coming their way. "Do you think it's time now for the fly-casting practice?" Jamie asked.

"Must be," said Max. "Yep, there's Grandpa, Mrs. Ellen, and Burt leading the way, all three carrying bamboo fly rods Grandpa made. There's Fred. There's Pat. He's Fred's best friend. They're carrying rings for people to cast their flies into."

"We know Pat. He's a neighbor and our ride back home," Jamie said.

"And you know his wife and little kid?" Max asked.

"Of course, we babysit for them sometimes. Love those Greek goodies she makes!" Joe said.

"We do too!" Max said.

"Back to the moment, are you going to try casting too?" Joe asked.

"Might watch the grown-ups first . . ."

"See how bad they are. Then try your luck," Jamie said, finishing Max's thought.

"Yeah."

"Good idea," Joe said.

"Maybe their voices will wake Charles. I know he's going to want to try. And while he's in line—sorry, bad pun. While he's waiting, I'll give you two a tree-fort tour," said Max.

And that is exactly what happened.

Chapter 8

Casting Out Lines

Four women, five high school and college guys, and ten older men gathered on a grassy spot near the pond. Fred and Pat placed three hula hoops of different sizes and colors far, farther, and even farther away.

"OK, I'm sure you can guess what the challenge is, but just in case, cast your line in a direct course so your fly falls into the ring you've picked," Fred announced.

It was like an arcade game without giant-sized stuffed toys, mirrors, rubber chickens, paintings of Elvis on velvet, or any of the usual prizes one wins. Instead, all casters would be applauded for their efforts. Later, those who landed inside a hula hoop ring would be awarded handmade dry flies made by Burt, Grandpa, or Mrs. Ellen.

Grandpa was up first to demonstrate how to cast a line.

"I'm using a little mayfly nymph I tied. I know it's hard

to see, but it's there. Nymphs are very popular with hungry trout looking for a snack," he explained before he began preparing for his first cast.

"He looks like a cowboy working a lasso to rope a steer, sheep, bull, or whatever they rope out West," Joe said.

"In the movie *Hatari!* John Wayne lassoed running rhino," Jamie added.

"Resource information from our resident video watcher," Joe said.

"We have that movie too," Max said. "I've watched it like maybe a hundred times."

"Anyway, back to the here and now. Look, see, it's not the bigger the loop the better. A big loop moves slower and, from what I've read, is a waste of energy when fishing," said Joe. "An expert fly-fishing dude named Lefty Kreh writes about casting and teaches classes, techniques in fly fishing. He says smaller loops are best and give you more energy to direct your fly where you want to place it."

"Too bad," Jamie said with a sigh. "I love seeing loops rolling all around in the sky like living creatures flying."

"That's because your element is air," Max said.

Jamie looked over at him and grinned. "Yep."

"Grandpa has complete control over his line. He pulls it off his reel, which is small enough to fit inside his hand," Max said. They watched as Grandpa, in fisher-person lingo, "stripped" off more and more line from the reel, guiding the free line between the fingers of his left hand.

"See the line in my hand?" Grandpa asked. "When you glide the line between your fingers, you are in better control. By holding your line like this, you better know when your fly is interesting Mr. Trout or Ms. Trout. And then you'll get to know each other well. You will feel and sense—almost—what they are feeling and thinking. When a fish wishes to run . . . let it. That's when your reel will spin. A fast fish swimming away makes a little reel spin as fast as if it were a spinning wheel spinning straw into gold like in the Grimms' tale . . . anybody remember?" he asked the group.

"'Rumpelstiltskin,'" a few voices called out.

"Exactly. There's no gold when fly fishing, but certainly, like the young woman in that classic tale, a good fisher person will outsmart a 'wise guy' trout by letting line race off your reel, and then with your hands, play the line. Sometimes you may have to crank slack back onto your reel," Grandpa said. He was still letting his rod stroke the sky as he let free more and more line.

"He's really taking his time," Joe whispered.

"I think he wants us to watch and see the rhythm of casting," Jamie answered.

"When he's ready, he'll let it drop," Max said.

Seconds after Max's comment, Grandpa used his entire arm and made a long cast. His homemade mayfly, tied to a barbless hook, raced silently through the air, dipped, and then fell right in the middle of the bright-orange hula hoop. It was the hoop placed farther away than any other, at least seventy-five feet.

Applause.

"Wow! Your grandpa is good," Joe said. "His fly landed in the center of that hoop on his first try."

"He's got a great eye," Max said proudly. "And experience. He's been fly fishing since he was about half my age."

Max looked back at the tree fort. He saw Charles climbing down the ladder.

"Charles is awake and ready to have a lesson," he told the others.

Fred, who was standing near them, overheard. He looked back and waved his arm at Charles. He turned and said to Max, Jamie, and Joe, "He's just in time to watch another pro. Then he can stand in line for a lesson."

"Ellen's turn," Grandpa said, reeling in his line.

Mrs. Ellen moved up beside Grandpa. She slid off a sweater she'd been wearing and unbuttoned the cuffs to the long sleeves of her collared shirt and rolled them up to her elbows. She held the cigar-shaped cork handle of her own bamboo fly rod with her thumb tilted towards her body.

"OK, everyone, look how Ellen holds the rod firmly. She knows rod, leader, and line are your best friends when trout fishing. How you hold the rod and work the line is the secret learned after much practice," Grandpa said. "There are lots of fancy terms for how you work the line. The current popular term is 'backhauling.' What it really means is having control over loose line you pulled off your reel, drawing it in, and letting it free as you *silently* swish your rod through the air. Good fly fishers keep both hands busy all the time. When both hands are occupied with fishing, it's hard to scare off some buzzing mosquitoes or scratch the place where others have gotten you. Best to splash on some bug dope before you start."

"I usually fish deep holes in small streams," Ellen said. "In small places, I cast using my wrist. I fish for a bit and then sit and watch what's happening in the trees, woods, and water. But I know some folks who fish all day long or some who need powerful casts against wind or rough waves, and that's when the entire arm is used for best results. But only use your arm up to your elbow. Not this way, but this," she demonstrated. With each cast, she let loose more line.

Even listening intently, people only heard a whispering hum from the line and rod. Ellen's style was very similar to Grandpa's.

Ellen let out more and more line. She was 'double hauling.' Finally, she asked Grandpa, "Shall I try to place this Grey Ghost beside your tiny Mayfly Dun or into another ring?"

"Up to you, Ellen," he said, smiling. "Folks, do you see how Ellen allows her line to travel in front of her before she 'snaps' it back?"

Murmurs:

"Yes."

"Oh my!"

"Yeah."

"Not to spoil your thunder, Mr. Y., but instead of letting my Grey Ghost lie where your mayfly sat, I'll pick a different ring," Mrs. Ellen said.

Like Grandpa, Mrs. Ellen let out lots of line. Then, unlike Grandpa, she leaned to her right, allowing the line to fly not over her head but by her side. Then when she decided enough line was off the reel, she let her fly fall in the middle hoop to her far left. She beamed at Grandpa, who beamed back. "I had to get my fly under that imaginary limb over there," she laughed, pointing to the sky.

Applause.

"Now we've seen the best until maybe Burt decides to show his skills. While the adults are practicing, want a quick tour of the tree fort?" Max asked.

"Sure," said Jamie and Joe.

"I'll stay here," said Charles. "I want to take some notes as I watch them."

"All the math for making the perfect cast," said Max.

"Math?" Jamie asked.

"Your rod is a flexible lever making various arcs. Physics," Charles said.

"How old are you?" Joe asked.

"He's ten but in AP math and beginner physics," said Max.

"Cool!" Joe said, edging over to where Charles stood. "So you are going to watch and . . ."

"And put what I observe into an equation. Then apply the laws of the equation to how I cast when it's my turn."

"And the momentum?" Joe asked.

"The momentum created by the rod making a longer arc should make my cast better," Charles said. He sat down in the grass, facing the group lined up for their casting lesson. He took his pad and pencil from the saggy back pocket of his jeans.

"Huh," Joe said. "Uh, I think I'll check out the fort later. I want to see how Charles uses physics."

"Not a problem," Max said.

"Want to borrow a piece of paper?" Charles asked. "Or a pencil. I have extra."

"Sure," Joe said. He sat beside Charles.

"We'll be right back," said Max.

"Joe is a math and physics whiz. He wants to figure out the math behind the perfect cast too," Jamie whispered to Max.

"Then he and Charles are a good match," Max said. "Let's go. Race you to the tree fort!"

"Sure." She took off.

Jamie beat Max to the tree fort by several horse lengths. "Sorry. I should have warned you, I hold blue ribbons for sprint and cross-country."

"That's OK," Max said, catching his breath. "Over here . . . up the ladder . . . then you'll be . . . on the main floor of our tree fort."

There was a low wall around the entire first floor. Above the main floor, two thick tree limbs, one on the right, one on the left, branched out. On each there were ladders to higher limbs where one could sit as a "lookout." Max climbed up one to demonstrate, but Jamie stayed on the main platform. She was studying a rope she saw tied to a hook and a box to stand on. "What's this, Max?"

"Tarzan swing for quick exits."

Jamie unhooked the rope and climbed onto the box. "Like this?"

"Wait. I'll show you," said Max, easing himself down from his crow's-eye perch to the main floor.

Jamie moved off the box to give him room. Max stepped onto the box. He placed his hands on the rope, in proper position, pushed his body forward, and lunged into the air. He swung out and back, back and forth, one, two, three times until he dropped his feet off the rope and let them drag on the ground to stop, stood, let go of the rope, and looked up at Jamie. "Like that. A bit scary, but if you take it easy . . . and if you've ever climbed a rope swing in school or somewhere, it isn't too hard."

"We've had lessons climbing ropes in gym for years," Jamie said. She knelt down and reached for the rope.

Max handed it to Jamie and stepped out of her way. He watched as she showed skills at swinging. Her thick red hair filled puffier and puffier with swing wind and blew behind her like a fuzzy parachute. He saw happiness on her face. *She's definitely in her element*, Max thought.

After Jamie had swung four or five times, Max said, "I know, lots of fun, but we'd better take a fly-casting lesson, don't you think?"

"Yes, I guess," said Jamie. "This has been terrific. When I was swinging, I imagined myself as different creatures flying through the air—an enchanted dragon minus nasty teeth and smoky breath, an angel lost en route back to wherever angels go after Christmas, or maybe my own guardian angel following me around? The possibilities are endless, don't you think?"

"Definitely, endless," Max said.

By the time they'd rejoined the fly-casting group, people were watching Charles as he showed his casting techniques. He held the rod and double hauled, as he'd been shown, worked his wrist, and made the line flow over his head before letting a fly drop into the nearest ring.

"Good job, Charles!" cheered Grandpa, Mrs. Ellen, Jamie, and Max.

"Easy?" Joe asked.

"Not really," said Charles. "Takes practice. You're next."

Joe reread his notes. Checked the physics formula he'd written down and stepped up.

"Want this rod or one of the new fiberglass ones?" Grandpa asked.

"I'll try the fiberglass," Joe said.

"It'll be light and fast," Charles warned. "You might need to rework your formula."

"Just get to know this rod. Make friends with it. Practice moving your wrist before you begin letting out line," Grandpa instructed.

Joe took the rod. Immediately a serious look scrunched his face. It was lighter than any fishing rod he'd ever used before, which meant its action would be very different. He was in front of people watching. An audience, but Joe had been put on the spot in other places and at other times before. He remembered all he'd read, all he'd seen, and he did as Grandpa suggested: he took his time getting to know the fiberglass rod, how to hold it and make it work. Finally, he began slowly stripping line from the reel. When he saw the forward cast go out as far as he wished and the back cast also do the same, his confidence grew. He remembered the formula he'd written down, revised it in his head, and applied it to how to cast with that fiberglass rod.

"Good," Grandpa said.

"I think you've got it. 'By George, you've got it,'" Max encouraged, borrowing from a song he'd sung in the school-musical version of *My Fair Lady*.

"It's feeling pretty OK," Joe said.

"Ready now to try to flip that fly inside a ring?" Fred asked him.

"Yeah," Joe said. "I mean, I guess."

"Go for it, Joe," Jamie whispered.

Joe stripped off more line and then backhauled some in. He kept his eye focused on one particular plastic hula hoop. After more "back and forwards," he let the leader, with a tiny streamer fly tied at its end, drop. It landed inside the ring he'd been aiming for.

"Wow!" he said. His heart was beating as if he'd run a race. He'd done it. He'd been challenged, and with careful study, in no hurry, he'd managed to place it just where he had wanted it to be.

He handed the fly rod to Grandpa, who shook his hand. "Well done, son!"

Fred slapped him on his back.

Jamie smiled.

Max and Charles made high fives.

Joe's face was radiant with his wide, happy grin.

Max and Jamie had their turns too. They each were able to sink their flies into hula hoop rings. Max needed more than one try. Jamie, like Joe, was a natural.

Max imagined, *Jamie feels it's she who is flying and not something tied to a leader and line.*

After the hula hoop target practice, the group moved

to the pond where Burt was ready to show everyone how to make a fly look alive on water. "A tempting snack to any fish looking for a 'goodie' to eat," Grandpa said.

"Strip out some line," said Burt. "See? I think that's enough. Let's let her down right . . . there." He let the leader, line, and fly land gently onto the still waters.

"Does that fly have a hook on it?" someone asked.

"Good question. It's a barbless hook. I'm sure no one wants to really catch a fish living here."

"What kind of fish are in there?" asked Joe.

"Most likely little bluegills," said Burt, making the fly "plip" and "pluck" upon the surface.

"How big are bluegills?" Jamie asked.

"Well now, usually a good-sized bluegill is six inches, but I've heard stories about people catching one or two in their lifetime that were a foot long. A twelve-inch-long bluegill would be quite a catch. But no matter the size, fishing for them is fun. For one thing, they're not picky eaters. They'll even go after bread crumbs if you just want to feed them. Today, hopefully, I can interest one. Then you'll see how they like to pluck and play."

Burt made the little fly "pop" and "plop" on the water. No action. He reeled in. "Let's try another spot."

Fred said, "No one wants to run the risk of hurting a pet bluegill. Burt's lesson to us is not about landing a fish, knocking it on its head, and taking it home for the frying pan. His lesson is all about the fake fly on your leader, how to make something *not* alive *look* alive as it moves on the water."

Burt cast into another place. "See, you have to twitch it," Burt said. "Then you let it sit."

"How long?" someone asked.

"Oh, not long. Twiddle it a few times. Make it look like it's gurgling," he laughed. "Skip it a bit. Let it sit. You see, this fly-fishing sport is not like tossing a red-and-white bobbin into the water and then sitting back in a boat or on a lake bank, snacking on the lunch you brought and waiting for something to happen. And then, maybe, having the bobbin disappear, pulled under by a king-sized fish who was going after the big fat night crawler skewed to a hook and sunk deep—a juicy dinner for some hungry monster."

"No?"

"No. Fly fishing is the game of making something created of feathers, threads, or hair—with maybe painted head, eyes, or nose—look like it's a living, or dying, insect lying on the water." He pulled the line in, slowly reeling it. He cast it into another area of the pond, not far from where the cattails grew. It was a shady spot.

"Let's see if anyone is hungry over in this hidden place," he said, working rod and line to make the imitation fly flit upon the water.

This time, there was a reaction from below. A great circling swirl plucked and wrinkled waves all around the fly. Then the fly disappeared.

"Ah, a customer! Now we wait and see how long before this critter discovers my fly doesn't taste so sweet. My fly will be, we hope, a big disappointment." Burt let out some line when the tip of the rod began bending and pointing down. "See? Some little guy has my fly and is swimming away. I've got to let out more line and wait to see what happens. Hopefully he's not swallowed my nicely tied, fancy mayfly, a gift from Mr. Y," Burt said.

As he said this, the rod bounced back up and the line went slack.

Burt began reeling. Soon, rocking like a pendulum on a tiny, tiny clock, the fly could be seen swaying a few inches below the rod's tip.

"Success," said Burt. "You saw how the artificial mayfly looked alive. You saw how the rod and line looked when a fish was momentarily fooled. I hope you all enjoyed some fun playing a game with a fish, and sharing the joy of getting your favorite fly back *and* knowing no one was hurt. That, my friends, is what fly-fisher people like to do. Oh sure, it's great to land a fish in your net, to hold it up for a photo shoot. But then let it swim free again to live and be a much wiser fish. That's the philosophy and the rule when you become a fish-for-fun, catch-and-release fly fisher. Now, who wants to try?" He said, stepping to one side. Many tried their talents at casting—"twitching, plipping, plucking"—and trying to convince the ever-wiser fish that their tiny bits of fur, feathers, and thread were living creatures.

Jamie had luck, while Joe and Charles did not. Max chose to watch.

Jamie gets it right away, but then she's really someone who understands air and has watched flying creatures for a long time. So of course she knows how to make her tied fly look real, Max thought. *If I was a fish checking out from my shadowy home below the skittering etchings on the quiet surface ceiling of my home, I might be tempted to investigate, look closer. And if my stomach was empty and growling, I might make a grab at even a tiny tidbit-sized nymph.*

Max and Jamie were "kind." They didn't tease Joe and Charles. *However,* Max thought, *it takes more than knowing the math and physics behind making a splendid cast when it comes to luring and trying to convince some fish what you're offering is really a living insect.*

After about an hour, Mrs. Ellen called, "Break!"

"Huh?" was the murmuring through the gathered group.

"Free time for, let's say, fifteen minutes. Then Mr. Y., Burt, and I will begin fly-tying workshops for any who are interested."

Chapter 9

Feathers, Fur, and Fun
Tying Flies 101

Jamie, Joe, Max, and Charles divided up. Each went to a different person to have a try at tying fly-fishing flies.

Mrs. Ellen was making Grey Ghosts and White Ghosts. Jamie went to work with her.

Burt was tying mayflies. Joe decided he wanted to make one after his experience casting.

Grandpa was making a Fan Wing Coachman. Charles liked the name, so he went to Grandpa's table.

Fred and Pat together were showing people how to turn coffee beans into little brown beetles. These were easy fishing bugs they'd learned how to make from Grandpa. Max knew this would be a fun project, but two things made him not sit down:

    1. There was no room. A group of eight people of
all ages, men and women, had gathered, and more

were dragging over chairs to sit, as close as possible, to learn how coffee beans could become beetles. Max noticed most were carrying cups filled to the brim with hot coffee.

2. Max could shrug his shoulders and walk away because he already knew how to make coffee-bean beetles. Grandpa had taught him a few months before on one "snow day" when school was cancelled. Max had been bored, sitting around the house at home, and skied down the hill to his grandparents' for hot cocoa, cookies, and a visit with Grandpa, who was making coffee-bean beetles. It had been a great afternoon, and Max had filled an empty baby food jar with the beetles he'd made.

Instead, Max decided he'd learn how to tie flies from Mrs. Ellen. He arrived at her table and found, besides Jamie, another person he knew. It was Grandpa's friend Chuck, a thin, quiet teacher Max liked.

"Max, you've decided to light here?" Chuck asked. "I'll move over to give you space. Ellen was waiting a few moments in case there'd be any late arrivals."

"And now I can begin," Mrs. Ellen said. "Today we'll make two streamers, a Grey Ghost and a White Ghost, both originally created by Carrie G. Stevens, a hatmaker gal from Vienna."

"Vienna?" Max interrupted. "Like Vienna in Europe or Maryland? I've been to Vienna, Maryland. That's where I had a great snapping-turtle adventure."

"No, Max, actually Vienna, Maine," Mrs. Ellen laughed. "She was born in Vienna and then, hang on and listen. She met her husband in Mexico . . . Mexico, Maine. You see, Maine has many towns named after very famous places."

"Wow. I've been to Maine too, but never Mexico," Max said.

His thoughts wandered off to a memory of his vacation in Maine, how twelve-year-old Zipper, the girl from Isle au Haut, showed him how creatures swim in tidal pools. *I wonder how Zipper is,* he thought. *I should send her a note and let her know we'll be traveling to Deer Isle, Maine, again this summer. Only thing is . . . I don't know when it will happen. Not sure what our vacation schedule is.*

Max noticed Mrs. Ellen looking at him, waiting for his thoughts to return back to the present moment. "Did Carrie G. Stevens live near Maine's coast?" he asked.

"No, she lived inland. Maine is a very wet state with many streams, ponds, lakes, and rivers. Carrie G. Stevens married a Maine Guide. Eventually they wandered into Northwestern Maine to a place called Great Falls, where her husband began his job as a fishing guide. Carrie G. was a hatmaker. Just imagine those ladies' hats back then! Ladies who had bobbed their hair short and stylish needed something fancy to wear. Some straw hats were dyed in colors advertised using names like 'glowing golden wheat' and many other flower colors."

"Really?" Chuck asked.

"Oh my, yes," said Mrs. Ellen. She struck a dramatic pose. "A straw hat dyed in orchid, golden wheat, or coral pink. Hat ribbons and cloth twisted and knotted to look like different types of flowers. One I especially loved, my grandmother's, had four blue roses made of taffeta that swung down from behind her ear to her shoulder. Very chic. Hats were also dressed with many types of feathers, which I imagine were the kinds Carrie G. Stevens made. Roaming the fields and woods, she probably gathered many from wild birds—blue jays, grouse, and pheasants—and mixed them with her own barnyard chicken and goose feathers. Hats decorated with peacock feathers were all the rage."

"Peacocks in Maine? " Jamie asked.

"Actually, yes, there were. A man who lived on Peacock Hill from late 1770s into the 1800s raised them," Chuck said. "You never know what you might find in Maine."

"Carrie G. Stevens used peacock feathers for fancy hats, but she also discovered other ways to use them."

"She used them in fishing flies?" Max asked.

"Yes, she did," said Mrs. Ellen. "But before we get to that part of the story, let me describe her. She was a woman who liked to sit by a stream, watching insects gathering. All those hours of watching turned into scheming—how to make tiny insects using material scraps left over after making her hats. She asked her husband, and he gave her some hooks. She had a clamp to hold a hook in place so her hands would be free." Mrs. Ellen pointed at her own free-standing clamp. "Then she put the hook in the clamp . . . like this," Mrs. Ellen demonstrated. "And began covering it with red thread. Next she added hair from a whitetail deer fawn." Mrs.

Ellen picked up a few hairs. "And some golden feathers."

All the time Mrs. Ellen talked, she was making a fly. They watched as she picked tiny bits from little piles of ingredients and tied them in place. Five tiny pieces of peacock tail were added on top of some yellow hairs and silver feathers for wings. This complicated fly had "jungle cock feathers for eyes" and "for a head, more black thread."

"Jungle cocks are roosters. Their normal habitat is India. They have beautiful feathers that are perfect for many fly-fishing flies, used sparingly," Chuck said.

When Mrs. Ellen was done, the fly she'd made looked more like a piece of art to be hung in a gallery than something one would cast out into the water as a fish lure. It was delicate and lightweight, and looked almost alive.

Jamie, Max, and Chuck murmured.

"Wow!"

"Jeez!"

"Super!"

"It's beautiful. Good job, Ellen," Chuck said.

"Thank you. Yes, not too bad. Needs to have two coats of what we call 'cement' over its head. But do you want to hear the rest of Carrie G. Stevens's story?"

"Yes."

"Of course."

"Please."

"Well then," Mrs. Ellen said, "Carrie G. Stevens named her fly a Grey Ghost. I'm not sure why. Then she went off to the stream to see if she could catch anything with it."

"Did she?" Jamie asked.

"Did she ever!" said Chuck.

"Yes, let's just say the floodlights of fame beamed on Carrie G. and her Grey Ghost fly when she caught a six-pound, thirteen-ounce brook trout on it. She took second prize in the *Field & Stream* contest," Mrs. Ellen said. "A proud moment for women back in the year 1924."

"Yippee," Jamie shouted.

"And the White Ghost?"

"I'm not sure when she designed it, but as you can see, it is softer, mostly white, and is, well, it is very ghostly," Mrs. Ellen said. "Carrie G. Stevens became a famous fly tier, tying many flies for many, many people. She had a long, successful life and died at an old age in 1970. But enough history, who wants to try to tie their own Grey or White Ghost? I have enough clamps for three to tie, and I count one, two, three of you here. Ready?"

For the next hour, Jamie, Max, and Chuck worked at tying flies, discovering just how hard it was to do something Mrs. Ellen had done so quickly. After an hour, they each had their own flies and a sense of pride in their work.

"But fish with this?" Jamie whispered to Max. "Never. I'm going to hang them from some almost-invisible threads and let them fly in my bedroom at home. There I can watch them whenever I want and imagine, or maybe even remember, what it feels like to fly."

Chapter 10

Plans for the Rest of the Day Are Announced

Joe, Charles, Jamie, and Max had gathered together to show each other the fishing lures they'd made. What a difference: colorful, furry, feathery, and fluffy, and the brown, oval coffee-bean beetles with tiny black thread legs, which made them all laugh when bounced inside the palms of their hands.

"Hello, you all. How's it going?" asked Pat, coming over to them.

"Great," they said.

"Good, good. OK, so let me put before you four a plan for the rest of your Saturday. First I'll let you know, it has been approved by both grandmas, your grandpa, your mom, Fred, and me."

"Okaaaay."

"Charles and Max, Fred and your mom want to take

baby Carrie out tonight to visit some friends, have dinner with them, then pick you guys up on their way home. Jamie and Joe, I'll be your driver home. Your grandmother has already been warned, just kidding. She's been called, and it was her suggestion that you invite a few friends over for dinner. She's cooking." Pat paused.

"Let me get this straight," Charles said. "Max and I are going someplace other than home and will be 'babysat' by someone other than Ralph and his longtime girlfriend, T. L. Toni?"

"That's the idea," Pat said.

"Oh, I get it," Jamie said. She looked at Joe. "Do you?"

"Uh yeah, I mean, oh, I guess it's up to Jamie and me to say, 'Hey, guys, want to come have dinner at our house, hear some cicadas singing their seventeen-year swan songs, and get a tour of Roland Park?'"

"Cool!" said Max and Charles.

"Then it's a yes from all four of you?" Pat asked. "Just making sure."

"Yep, yes."

"Yes."

"For sure."

"Yes, but do Charles and I have time to, uh, you know, change out of these sort of fishy clothes and into something less slimy?" Max asked.

"Yes, you can run up now. We'll give you thirty minutes to clean up. Then be here, say, by four and I'll take all of you into THE BIG CITY!" Pat said. "I'll meet you by the cement porch. I need to let Fred know you've all OK'd the adult plans." He walked away.

"And while you guys are gone, Joe and I will help your grandma and whoever else is in the kitchen to clean up," Jamie suggested.

"Is that fair?" Max asked. "I mean, leaving you guys to work while we get cleaned up?"

"Oh yeah, it is," said Joe. "Because when we get back to our house and Jamie and I need to clean up because we're all fishy slimy too, you can help our grandmother with dinner. Then afterwards we'll show you all our favorite haunts in Roland Park." He looked at Jamie and grinned.

Jamie grinned back. "Sure."

"We'll even take a stroll over to 'The Morgue,'" Joe said with a grin.

Halfway up through the pony pasture, Charles grabbed Max by his shirtsleeve.

"Yeah?" Max asked. He stopped and turned to look at Charles.

"OK, Mr. Dictionary, just fact checking, but did Joe say we'd walk over to 'the morgue' just now?"

"Yeah, that's what he said," said Max.

"And a morgue is . . . I mean, doesn't it have something to do with dead people?" Charles's face was so scrunched up it looked like a wet dish towel twisted and wrung before someone would toss it dry and flat.

"Yeah, it's where they take bodies when they need to do some . . . research on them to figure out why they died, or maybe it might be a body someone finds and they need to check out what killed them and who they might be," Max said. He had been working his imagination away from thinking too much about what Joe had said.

"Maybe Joe's got the idea we like science stuff and I'd like to see what kind there is near where they live?" Charles asked.

"Hey, look, don't sweat it, Charles. We've been hanging around with Joe and Jamie all day, and it's been cool, right?"

"Yes."

"I mean, I never once got the creeps from either one of them, did you?"

"No, not at all. Even Jamie is all right, for a girl," Charles said. His face was beginning to look relaxed.

"Right, so we just have to trust whatever this morgue thing is will be OK," Max said. He gave Charles a punch on his arm. "Race you to the shower!"

"You're on!"

Max and Charles ran as fast as each could to their house.

Running helped to erase all the scary images about dead stuff and buildings where bodies might be stored.

They both arrived at the back door together and flipped a penny on who would be first to shower.

They were back at their grandparents' house in less than thirty minutes.

"Twenty-nine minutes and fifty-one seconds, to be exact," Charles announced.

Chapter 11

Hillside Avenue and a Story

Pat's van became the transport vehicle for one ten-year-old and three thirteen-year-olds. It had two bucket seats up front, a middle bench seat sized to fit three, and another bench in the rear for four large adults, which Pat called "the way-back seat." All were equipped with seat belts.

Max chose the "way-back," took from his knapsack a pen and a journal, and began scribbling his entry for the day. Jamie sat in the passenger bucket seat. Joe and Charles shared the middle bench, continuing their discussion on the physics of fly fishing.

The van was "family clean" with half a dozen empty coffee cups rolling on floor mats, books piled on seats, and travel maps and music tapes stuck in door pockets. Compared to Fred's truck, it felt roomy. Max and Charles

felt almost at home. It was like their mom's van, minus a
Celtic music tape playing. Instead of soft, throbbing harp
strings, Pat's radio was tuned to a rock station, volume on
low. U2's "I Still Haven't Found What I'm Looking For,"
followed by a song called "(I've Had) The Time of My
Life," filled the empty spaces around them. All felt relaxed
and comfy riding on back-country roads. Then Pat turned
the volume lower and announced, "We'll take the scenic
way back, down Hillside Avenue. Who knows, we may
even see a gray ghost."

Suddenly the atmosphere inside the van changed.

"You mean a fishing fly hanging from a tree limb
someone lost in a bad cast?" Joe asked.

Pat laughed. "No, I mean the Ghost of Hillside Avenue.
Nobody here in this van knows about her?"

Silence, followed by four voices in unison saying, "No."

"Wow, crazy. Max, you and Charles have traveled on
Hillside Avenue before, right?" Pat asked.

"Oh yeah, it's one of the back roads Mom and Fred take
to avoid traffic jams on the Jones Falls Expressway," Max
said. "But they never said there was a ghost near there."

"Well, there is. Many times, sad singing is heard in the
upstairs rooms of the Valley Inn Restaurant. But there's
more."

"Will you tell us?" Charles asked.

"Sure," said Pat. He reached over and turned off the
heavy metal beat, which had begun throbbing through
the van's speakers. "So I'll tell you the story as told to me
by a dear friend who heard it from a great-aunt, all who
claim every part is true."

The Gray Ghost Story Pat Told

On a misty late-May evening many years ago, a sixteen-year-old girl left her house to take a walk on a dirt lane, now paved and named Hillside Avenue. She was going to meet her twin sister at the train station. The station still stands, but now it's a private home. The flat bed where train tracks once ran is visible when you look through a narrow row of tall trees. One twin, Emmy, was returning home on the train from her job as nanny for a family who lived in Baltimore City. She made this trip every few months. It was a trip home to see her family. Her sister Mary always met her. They were identical twins who loved to trick people by pretending to be each other.

Emmy's train arrived on time. The night was lovely. From the marsh, tree-frog songs filled the quiet. The waning moon, no longer full, was a shadowy glow through the trees. The twins hugged each other. Mary took one of Emmy's travel bags, so each carried one. They began walking back to their parents' home on Hillside Avenue, holding hands and swinging them and talking, catching up on the latest news. You might wonder what year this was. It was 1910.

*They had stopped their talk to listen to frog ballads and the faraway calling of an owl when they saw
something shimmering,
something gray,*

something floating inches above the ground,
something coming towards them.

They spoke not a whisper, but each continued walking,
holding hands, and watching as the gray ghost, a woman
wearing a long, soft-and-flowing nightgown, came closer
and closer towards them.

Closer.

Closer.

Closer.

Emmy and Mary always told this story the same way to
all for the rest of their very long lives, the exact same story.

After seeing the gray ghost, they kept walking, but they
never spoke a word to each other until moments later,
when they arrived home . . . running, keeping pace with
each other. Then at their home and leaning against the
door, right before they entered, Mary and Emmy looked
at each other, and this is what they said:

Emmy: "She went right through our hands."

Mary: "And when she did, it felt like ice."

"Many days, weeks, months, and years, they often
walked Hillside Avenue, but never again did they do it

alone at night. And though they lived in their parents' house with their siblings, no one else in their family ever claimed to see the Gray Ghost again," Pat said.

"Has anyone else ever seen her?" Max asked.

"Some claim yes," Pat said. "Maybe many have seen her, but unlike Mary and Emmy, they haven't had the nerve to tell about their experiences. But, hmm, Max and Charles, tonight the moon is waning. It is the last day/night of May, warm and lovely. Tonight, if your mom and Fred happen to take Hillside Avenue, you just might see the Gray Ghost," Pat said.

"OK, here's where we turn onto Falls Road. Soon we'll cross the city line, and probably in about ten to fifteen minutes, depending on traffic delays, we'll be in Roland Park."

Pat switched the van's radio back on. Music from the Disney movie *The Great Mouse Detective* filled the van as all youth riders sat thinking about the story they had just heard, as their imaginations twisted and churned it into a story they'd remember for a long, long time.

Max wrote in his journal: *Maybe tonight, if we take Hillside Avenue home, we'll see something we'll never forget. More later.*

Chapter 12

Roland Park, Cicada Songs, "The Morgue," and More

Max, Charles, Joe, and Jamie listened to classic rock—Beatles and Carole King—turned down low for the rest of the trip while thoughts of the Hillside Avenue Gray Ghost bounced in their heads and tour guide Pat pointed at historic sites along the way.

"See these old stone houses? Once they were homes where workers who worked nearby in the grist mills lived. You all know what grist mills were?"

"Uh, maybe," said Joe.

"Huh?" asked Charles, stretching.

"Something used to grind things?" asked Jamie.

"Tell us, Pat," Max said.

"Baltimore County and Baltimore City had many grist mills. Some reports state as many as 365 all running at one time. In 1820, a historical essay states Baltimore was the lead flour-milling city . . . wait for it . . . *in the world,"* Pat said. He pointed at a river roaring beside the road. "This river was used by some."

"That's wild. Our city, famous for flour," Joe said.

"Baltimore was famous for many things. Flour, which was really important, was just one," Jamie said.

"It's famous for a writer of scary stories and poetry," Pat nudged.

"Edgar Allan Poe!" four voices said together.

"Yep, 'Quoth the raven . . .'"

"Nevermore!" the foursome crowed again.

"Caw!" Pat laughed.

"We went on a class trip there once, remember, Joe?" Jamie asked.

"How could I forget it? I even remember the address, #3 Amity Street. 'Amity' means when two people get along in a friendly way. Who did Poe have amity with? The house is made of brick, right, Pat?" Joe asked.

"Correct. Built in about 1833, Poe's aunt lived there, and quite a few others. As for 'amity,' a young woman lived there, who Poe later married."

They let Poe as a married man rest there. They were all more interested in buildings than some dusty old relationship.

"And the house is, like, really little. Talk about living in a tiny house," Joe said.

"Well, it is two and a half stories, but you're right, it's small. Historians have written that Poe lived on the top floor, under the slanting roof," Pat said.

"Poor Poe. I always feel sorry for him. He died when

he was kind of young, right?" Jamie asked.

"Well, he was born in 1809 and died in 1849, so yep, fairly young. Yes, he had a sad life," Pat said.

"Which is why he wrote sad poems and some really scary stories," Jamie said.

"'The Pit and the Pendulum,' 'The Black Cat,' and 'The Fall of the House of Usher,' to name a few scary-dreary masterpieces. OK, we'll leave Poe for now. There's lots more Baltimore history," Pat said.

"We read about the schooner trade, how Baltimore was one of the stops when schooners sailed from Maine to Havana, Cuba," Max said.

"Excellent fact," Pat said. "And Baltimore is famous for a song sung at many ballgames," Pat said.

"'The Star-Spangled Banner'!" four voices yelled.

"Exactly. It was written by Francis Scott Key about the 1814 battle in Baltimore Harbor. Forts and cannons, 'and the rocket's red glare, the bombs bursting in air.' Great lyrics," Pat said.

"And we're heading to Roland Park, another historical spot. It was developed, so I've read, between 1890 and 1920 on something like 700 acres of land around beautiful Lake Roland, with streetcar access to the big city of Baltimore. Streetcars, hmm, they were like buses but ran on tracks, looked a bit like the car of a train. Plans for Roland Park included Victorian homes and many parks, some with streams and woods, and even, early on, they built a group of shops all strung together, which became known as the first planned shopping center. It is a great place to live, right? Jamie? Joe?"

"Yeah, it's pretty special. Except right now those seventeen-year cicadas are really singing up a storm," Joe said. "You guys just wait 'til you hear them here. You think they're loud at your house. Whew, anyway, just you wait." Joe said.

'*Henry Higgins, just you wait!*' Max thought, lyrics from the *My Fair Lady* song repeating in his head.

"We're close to home now. We're turning onto Roland Avenue, and soon we'll be at your house on . . ."

"Hawthorne," Jamie and Joe said together.

All looked at the large homes, most with big front porches, as the van drove by them. They saw many, many trees along the four-lane road, connecting lanes, and quiet dead-end streets. Except for asphalt surfaces and modern-day cars in driveways or sideways, one could almost imagine they'd entered another time in history, maybe even way back to 1900.

Within a few minutes, Pat slowed the van and parallel parked close to a sidewalk and in front of a yellow house with green shutters and gabled windows.

"This is it!" Jamie said.

"Home," said Joe.

Charles and Max looked and saw not one house but two joined together.

"Two houses?" Charles asked.

"It's called a duplex. We live in the one with the bright-red geraniums," said Jamie. "House on the other side is where a little old lady lives. She can be sort of grouchy, until she gets to know you. Then she's friendly."

"Well, friendlier," corrected Joe.

"Anyway, she lives in the other half of the duplex, but

lucky for probably all, Joe's bedroom and mine are on outside walls, nowhere near her rooms. We can play our radios and boom boxes with the volume up, and we can talk above a 'whisper.' But if we shared walls with her, she might be knocking on them for us to pipe down," Jamie explained. "Grandma's room is the biggest room on the second floor, and faces the street. She shares a wall, but she keeps her radio on the outside wall, just to be safe. Good to keep neighbors happy," Jamie explained.

"Like apartment living, only it's a whole house. *And* it's much bigger than Poe's house," Joe said.

"All out," said Pat.

As Max stared at the house, he saw a motion from inside. The front-door curtain was pulled back and someone looked out, and then immediately the curtain dropped. Within seconds, the door opened. A woman stepped out onto the gray-painted floorboards of the porch. She was smiling and waving her hand at them.

"Hi, Grandma!" Jamie and Joe called, climbing out of the van to the sidewalk and running to greet her. Pat, Max, and Charles got out of the van and followed the path, up the steps, and soon were on the front porch too. Jamie and Joe stepped aside to make room for them.

"Hello, all," Jamie and Joe's grandmother said. "Now, Pat, who do you have with you? Max and Charles, I bet."

"I'm Max," said Max.

"I'm Charles," echoed Charles.

"Wonderful to finally meet you, Max and Charles," she said as she shook hands with both. "You may call me Grandma J., if you wish."

"Hello, Grandma J.," said Max.

"Hi," Charles said.

"I have dinner cooking. It won't be done for about one and a half hours. Jamie and Joe, why not show Max and Charles the trail down to Stoney Run, unless you're all tired out from your fly-fishing event."

"Sure, Grandma," said Jamie. "But we'd like to clean up first. Is that OK?"

Grandma looked carefully at Jamie and Joe. She wrinkled up her nose and then laughed. "Yes, well, you both do look—and smell—as if you've been on a fishing adventure. Why don't you clean up while I show Max and Charles our backyard? Coming, Pat?"

"Love to, but expecting company in about . . ." He looked at his watch. "Fifteen minutes. I'd best hurry home and wash too, or my dear, patient wife might not be pleased with me," Pat said.

"Understood," Grandma J. said.

"See you all," Pat said, heading back to the van.

"Bye, Pat! Thanks so much!" Jamie, Joe, Max, and Charles said in chorus.

"My pleasure. Don't forget, Max and Charles, when you're traveling home tonight with your parents, keep your eyes peeled back for unusual sights."

"Yes, sir," Max and Charles said in voices not as enthusiastic as before.

Grandma J. opened wide the front door and allowed the four ahead of her. Jamie and Joe raced up a staircase that was off the entrance hall. "See you soon!" Jamie called out.

"Right this way to the back garden," Grandma J. said, leading them through the living room, into a dining room where a big table was set for five, and then through a large warm and sweet-smelling kitchen. She opened the door to the back porch. Within minutes, they were outside again, where they found a large, round black iron table with many matching chairs. On the table sat an icy-cold metal pitcher and a stack of multicolored tin glasses. Beyond the roof-sheltered back porch was a long, grassy yard framed on each side by blooming spring flowers.

This is not the yard I expected to find when Jamie and Joe told us they lived in Baltimore City, Max thought.

"I just filled this pitcher with lemonade. Anyone thirsty?" Grandma J. asked.

"Gee, thanks," Charles said.

"Yes, thank you," said Max.

"Pick your favorite colored glass and I'll fill it."

After their glasses were filled, everyone found places to sit where they could look at the yard. All around them, they heard the loud chorus of cicada songs.

"All day and usually all night, except when it drops below seventy degrees, we've had cicada music this late spring, and it will continue into summer. According to what I've read, it'll last about two months. I'm glad this doesn't happen every summer. It's special, but to be honest, I prefer concerts at Symphony Hall, where I sit down and music comes and goes between friendly chatter, silence, and applause," Grandma J. said. "Maybe next time you two visit here, it'll be a more usual nature time of year and not during seventeen-year cicada songs."

"Have you lived here long?" Max asked.

"In Roland Park? Oh my, yes, I was born on Edgevale Road. It was big and very roomy even with all my sisters and brothers, seven of us in all when counting my parents. But this house," she said, waving her hand around towards the yellow house and yard, "this house is where I moved when my husband and I married. That was many years ago."

"You've always lived in Roland Park?" Charles asked.

"Always. Oh my, now I'm telling my age. I was born in 1924, in the middle of the Roaring Twenties. I have a few early memories of my mom and daddy all dressed up and going out to parties. My mom loved hats filled with peacock and pheasant feathers, and flowers made from tulle and silk lining their bands. I remember my parents both looked quite smashing. Then the stock market crashed in '29. Most of my memories are of the Great Depression. Our family was lucky. We lived simply. My father had never put his money in banks. He kept it hidden in safes inside the house, and he had a job where they would always need him. He worked for the fire department. Since our house was big, we let out rooms to some people. We kids doubled up, but it was OK, and my parents took in others who were struggling. Everyone worked together doing chores, cooking meals. I went to the local State Teacher's College in Towson and in three years was employed teaching. Teaching is something I've always done and always enjoyed doing, especially third and fourth grades. I like teaching almost as much as swimming. That's a big almost. I love swimming."

She's tall, thin, muscular, tanned, and pretty. Even if her hair is silver-gray, she looks lots younger than she is, Max thought.

"Every summer vacation, I close up the house, pack up Jamie and Joe, and off we go to Ocean City, where I swim in the ocean. But I swim in any water considered swimmable—in quiet waters of a pond or lake, or by tubing on a river. I love water."

"I'm a swimmer too," Charles said. "My stroke is the butterfly."

"He's really good," Max said. "We have a wall covered with ribbons and shelves of trophies as evidence." Max was proud of his swimming-champ brother.

"Wonderful!" Grandma J. said. "I used to compete when I was your age. My best stroke is the front crawl. I never mastered the butterfly. Good for you," Grandma J. said.

"Are you near water here?" Charles asked.

"Oh my, yes. When Jamie and Joe arrive and after they've had their lemonade cooler, I'll suggest a walk down to Stoney Run."

"We'll do that!" they heard. Within seconds, Jamie and Joe appeared on the porch.

"Wonderful," Grandma J. said, standing up. She took the pitcher and poured each twin a glass of lemonade. "Seconds?" she asked Max and Charles.

"No, thanks," said Max, "but it tastes great."

"I'll take seconds with dinner, if that's OK," Charles said.

"That's fine," Grandma J. said. "And maybe after dinner,

Jamie and Joe, you'll take the boys on one of the little paths. Sunset Path might be fun. Here in Roland Park, Max and Charles, I think you'll feel almost like you're in the country. It was planned to be that way—to be a community where hills, dales, forests, streams, and all wonderful wildwood wonder lands were important. Builders added paths, roads, and houses. Instead of bulldozing all of the trees down to build houses and then hiring gardeners to plant new foliage, they left the old growth. Makes sense, right?"

"Right," they said.

"Except because there have been no big machines here in the last seventeen years, the woods have not been disturbed except maybe by barking dogs, music, and people having loud conversations. Old growth rewards us with this amazing cicada singing event every thirteen or seventeen years," Grandma J. said. "Any math whizzes here?"

"Charles and Joe," Jamie and Max said.

"OK, you two," Grandma J. said. "What do numbers thirteen and seventeen have in common?"

"Both are uneven numbers," Charles said.

"True, but there's more," Grandma J. nudged.

"Oh, I know," said Joe. "They're both prime numbers, right?"

"Exactly," Grandma J. said. She clapped her hands. "And a prime number is?"

"A number that can only be divided evenly by one and itself," Joe said, rattling off the textbook definition he'd memorized, "and it has to be larger than one."

"Excellent. So just a funny little fact, the biggest, loudest cicada years are the prime-number years of thirteen or seventeen. In other words, there is a noisy group of cicadas visiting us every thirteen years and another whole group or strain appearing every seventeen years. What both have in common, besides being prime numbers, is they are especially loud and plentiful. OK, enough science and math for now."

"I've heard some people refer to cicadas as locusts, but that's not correct, right?" Max asked.

"Correct, a locust is actually a grasshopper. You can even find those rascals mentioned in the Old Testament as one of the many plagues. But Bible lessons are for Sunday school teachers and preachers, not for the likes of a public school third-grade teacher like me." She shook her head. "OK, Jamie and Joe, do you remember the shortcut to Stoney Run?"

"Hawthorne to Keswick, and from there we'll find Stoney Run," Jamie said.

"Good! Looks like it's showtime!" Grandma J. looked at her wristwatch. "See you all in one hour for dinner."

Walking on a wooded trail, Max and Charles passed more houses than they would have at home, but each house had a big shady yard and gardens. Some had high wooden fences for privacy, but even those were stained in natural colors to blend in with nature's habitat.

The trail meandered left, right, down, and up through grassy places where purple, pink, and white tiny wildflowers were blooming.

"It is almost like at home," Max said.

"Except for traffic on the road over this hill in front of us," Joe said.

"Hey, look over here," Jamie said. She was standing in front of a massive old tree.

"What?"

"Huh?"

"Find one?"

"Come and look," Jamie said.

Soon the boys were standing close beside Jamie, looking to where she pointed. Then they saw. Not one. Not two. But five . . .

"Empty shells. See? There's a crack down the back of each one."

"They all look identical," Charles said.

"They pretty much are," said Joe. Very carefully he took a shell off the tree bark.

They all examined it. It was amber colored, light as a chickadee feather, and there was a slit down its back. "That's where the cicada squirmed out. Over time, its wings dried and it was able to fly away from its old husk in search of a mate," Jamie said.

"This cicada shell is made of special stuff. Its fancy, scientific name is 'chitin,' which means it's actually a kind of glucose—or, one might say, sugar. Anyone need a candy fix? There're plenty of shells here to crunch on. Yum," Joe said. "All true. We had a science lab last week on these guys and gals."

"Cool facts," Max said.

"Yeah, we can wow some of our class in school, right?" Charles said, looking at Max.

"Maybe," Max said, his mind still stuck on the slit in the shell. "You know, this squeezing out of a chitin shell can't be easy. Do any die at that stage?"

"Probably," Joe said. "You guys want to know the cicada life cycle? It's actually pretty amazing."

"Sure."

"Go for it, Joe." Max took out his pencil and notepad.

"Well, let's use this shell and go backwards and forwards. Seventeen years ago, the mama cicada found a protected groove in the barky shadows on a big tree. There she laid her eggs, which look a lot like rice grains. When first hatched, the cicada looks like a termite. It sucks on the fluids in the tree. It gets stronger and bigger. When it is ready to leave its own tree groove, it wriggles down the tree until it's on the ground. It needs to be near tree roots because the tree is its healthy beverage machine, always. But once it finds the perfect place—earth beside good tree roots—then it bores itself a tunnel where it will spend many years. It will continue tunneling and feeding for up to seventeen years." Joe was smiling. "Some story, huh?"

"Yep."

"Yeah."

"Oh, Joe, such a good storyteller," Jamie said. "Our science teachers told us last week that we can also call this shell a 'nymph exoskeleton.' After a cicada is done living in its deep earthy tunnel, it emerges as a nymph. Then it climbs the tree and, as soon as possible, cracks free of its shell. The rest of the story is fly, find mate, and sing songs in a chorus, like what we are hearing now. Should a bunch of cicadas panic, it is . . . well, let's just say the sounds are not so pretty. More like an 'Ah-O! Ah-O! Ah-O!' instead of a very loud musical maraca, multiply one maraca into hundreds all playing at the same time until the air cools down. Like when it gets to be about seventy degrees, then they quiet down. Oh, and the music is made by the guy cicadas trying, you know, to charm the ladies. Lady cicadas make sounds too . . . the sound of wings flying through the air."

"Wow!" Max and Charles said together.

"Always got to blame it on the guys," Joe said, laughing.

Jamie mocked a bow and then laughed. "I've been studying. I have a test on this on Monday."

"Looks like maybe an A," Max said.

"Not quite, I can't remember the name for the male cicada's body part that makes the noise."

"It has a name? Ugh, I forget it too," Joe said. "Mature nymph cicadas are called imagoes, that much I remember. And also, the males can make so much noise because the females are filled with eggs that need to be, you know . . ."

"Yeah, females' bodies are so filled with eggs that they have no room to play music except by flying with their lovely wings," Jamie said.

"Lovely?" Charles asked.

"Well, to another cicada," laughed Joe.

"Hey, give them a break. Think how amazing they are, and unlike us. They even have five eyes," Jamie said.

"Five? I thought only two big red ones," Charles said.

"No, Jamie is right. They have five eyes. One on each

side and three little ones in the center, which they use for detecting light and darkness. Another odd fact but good to know, they do not always have red eyes. Some cicadas have white, gray, blue, yellow, and even multicolored eyes. Scare you?" Joe said, laughing.

"Wow," said Max. "I knew they were noise makers. I knew that other animals ate them and that fish really loved them, but I never knew all this stuff about them. I'll be ready if our school does a science unit on them this week, or whenever. I've been taking notes." He held up his notepad.

"Max has the facts," Charles said.

"Max the Facts Guy. Nice," Jamie said. She smiled at him.

"Yeah, cool, right?" Joe said. "Now I can admit to you my feelings about these critters. Look around the roots. See? There are the holes they crawled out of when they were climbing into the light after seventeen years of darkness." Joe was down on his knees, trying to look as far into each hole as he could. "Imagine living down in there all those years."

"Darkness," Max said

"Bored," said Charles.

"Listening to earth sounds, you think?" asked Jamie.

Joe sat back on his heels, looked at the others, and then said, "You know, I've been thinking all afternoon. Well, on and off, about what Burt said to us about portals, how each of us has our own way to enter nature. And you, Jamie, and you, Max," he said, looking at each, "you both found yours, while Charles and I needed more time to explore and think about it. Back at your place, near the pond, before we went for casting and fly-tying lessons, I was looking around an old black walnut tree. I felt a twinge, like I began to get it, but I still wasn't sure. I really wasn't sure until just now. And now I know," Joe said. He gave a big smile. Like a smile one has when they're satisfied with something they've made.

"So are you going to tell us?" Charles said impatiently. "He looked at his watch. "I mean, we do have to make it back in time for dinner in about twenty-two minutes."

"Don't sweat it, Charles, we have plenty of time," Jamie said.

Max glared at Charles. "Come on, Charles, this is not a time to second off. Joe has something to share that's important."

Charles blushed. "Sorry," he said to the others. He turned to Joe. "Sorry, Joe."

"That's OK, Mr. Time Guy. I get it," Joe said. "I'll make it short. I have this thing for burrows. I mean, I always have liked to read storybooks and then nature books about creatures burrowing down below the surface. When I was little, Grandma read us *The Wind in the Willows*."

"Our mom read it to us. I love that book," Max said. "Charles, remember?"

"Yeah, the battle to win back Toad Hall was really cool," Charles said.

"The wind blowing through the willows," Jamie said. "Oh, those great picnics Ratty made, and how Mole loved his time out of his own little hole, free and exploring the greater world of adventure."

"All true," said Joe. "But what I loved best *were* those burrows. What I wanted most was to have one of my own. Someplace where I could burrow right down in a hole in the ground. This year in school science classes, our teacher was right on target teaching us about these little guys."

Joe stood up and pointed at the amber-colored empty cicada shell. "The whole life journey of these amazing insects is something that has kept me focused in school this spring. Look at all these holes. Man, they're everywhere. Just think, one hole with a cicada in it for all those years, what did he or she do? What did he or she feel? I mean, if cicadas feel. What did he or she think about? If cicadas think at all. Or to put it another way, what would I do, feel, and think if I was living in a burrow for seventeen years, hearing my own heartbeat, winding my own clock, Charles, and listening to the tick-tocks? So, I guess, what all this means is, I'm someone whose portal into nature is asking questions and looking for answers concerning the things of the earth."

"Oh, Joey," Jamie said in a tone only a twin sister could use, "I'm glad you know now. I think it will help you . . . you know, in all kinds of ways." She gave him a hug, which he accepted.

"Yeah, I think so too, twin sister who dreams of wings."

Max and Charles had turned away to give the twins a moment. "Hey, over here, look! I see more," Charles said after about sixty seconds had passed.

They found many amber-colored shells with back-split openings. They eased a few off the places where they were attached to tree bark.

Wow, they feel crisp, Max thought. He watched Charles hold one up to the sun. Max tried it too. *The sun coming through this little shell makes it glow.*

"Have you all looked at these shells like Charles is doing?" he asked.

"Many times," Joe said.

"Yep," said Jamie. "I've also looked at the little split where they emerged and thought about, sadly, the ones who never got out, the ones who for some reason got stuck."

"Have you seen those too?" Max asked.

"Yep," said Jamie. As if to herself, she added, "they never flew. They never finished their life goals."

Like your parents and grandfather dying in a horrible plane crash, Max thought. *Growing up, you discover more ways and many more people who have had their lives changed in only a few moments.* He shook his head, *time to be in the moment and enjoy the now.* He looked through the little amber shell at the sun again. *At least the one who lived in this shell got out and flew away.*

"OK, you all," said Joe, checking his watch. "We'd better run. Dinner will be served in ten minutes."

Off they ran as if all four were flying.

"Here we go! We're in running-fast, flying mode. Imagine we've all turned into cicadas!" yelled Jamie.

They made buzzing noises, imitating happy cicada songs.

They arrived exactly in time to wash up and then sat down to a great feast of mashed potatoes, green beans, juicy roast beef, and rolls "from Eddie's Market," Grandma

J. admitted. "Who can compete with the best?"

They shared with Grandma J. the events of the day, including the discovery of so many cicada shells. They kept secret the portals into nature details. Max and Charles had decided portal knowledge was something Jamie and Joe should share with Grandma J. when they felt the time was right. They would tell Mom and Fred about their portals when they felt it right to tell them.

Max was very aware Charles had yet to say what his portal was, if, in fact, he even knew. Max had an idea what it might be, but there was no way he would tell Charles. No, each person must discover their own portal, in their own time, through their own adventure.

After dinner, everyone helped with cleanup. Grandma J. washed dishes. Jamie and Max dried them. Charles carried clean dishes back to the dining room. Joe put them away all in their proper places. Group effort made the job fun, and everything was done in record time.

"7:15!" Grandma J. announced as the clock on a marble-top table chimed. "Now I'm scooting you all out the door so you can see what you might find on the Sunset Trail. You two know the way?"

"Grandma, you've only taken us there a hundred times," Joe said.

"And afterwards, before being back here by nine on the dot, you might . . ." Grandma said.

"Oh, we have it all planned. We're taking them to The Morgue," Jamie said, winking at Joe.

"Oh good," Grandma J. said. "Great plan. Max and Charles, I know you'll enjoy The Morgue. Have fun!"

Max was afraid to look at Charles. Actually he was afraid to look at anyone. Instead, he looked at the furniture in the living room. Then he focused on his feet as he followed Jamie and Joe through the house to the front porch and down the steps.

"This time, we have to cross the big highway," Jamie said.

"Be careful. You know the rules. Look both ways before you cross Roland Avenue. And cross at the crosswalks only," Grandma J. called after them.

"We will!" Joe called back.

They took Hawthorne to Oakdale to Roland Avenue, a two-lane "highway." Here they waited for cars to pass by standing safely in a wide, green grassy and flower-filled median strip. Once on the other side, they continued down Oakdale to Goodwood Gardens and then Club Road. Finally, Joe pointed at a wooden sign marked Sunset Trail.

"Here we are," he announced.

Max and Charles saw a well-worn rough path with places where they had to go down many steps. There were bushes, trees, and banks filled with blooming flowers. They passed many homes, including, as Joe pointed out, Rusty Rocks, a Tudor-style home once belonging to a Mr. Bouton.

"Mr. Bouton was one of the brains behind making Roland Park the special place it is," Jamie said.

The Sunset Path took them to a club. They could see grass cut to look like lovely rolling lawns and many places where people could gather.

"We're close to some of the private schools, and lots of students use this path if they want a shortcut to the Club. It's a fun place for sledding, cross-country skiing, or snowboarding. We've sort of grown up coming here."

"I cross-country ski and Joe snowboards, now that we are both *older*," Jamie added.

Joe ignored her and continued being a tour guide. "You can take Sunset Trail farther down to Falls Road to catch a bus or just to be . . . you know, *older teens*," Joe said. He looked at Jamie and shook his head.

I think Joe wants to take his time being a kid before turning fourteen. Ugh, I'll be fourteen in August. I'm not sure I'm ready for that yet, Max thought.

"Shall we head back?" Joe asked.

"Before the teen lovers start appearing on this path," Jamie added.

"Sounds like a plan," said Charles.

"Good idea," Max added.

The route back was different. "Don't want to bore you with the same sights," Joe said. "We'll take Beechdale to Long Lane, which will pop us out close to The Morgue."

Going back, they all noticed the shells and bodies of dead cicadas.

Were there this many bodies when we came, Max thought, *or do I have morgue fears and sights I might see erupting in my brain cells?*

"Most of these bodies will be gone by morning. All kinds of animals love to feast on cicadas—wild animals like raccoons, possums, and snakes, and tame pet dogs, even people. Ever try them?" Jamie asked.

"True confession time, Max," Joe laughed.

"We have," Charles said. "We've tried them many ways. We even thought, once upon a time, like two days ago, of having a stand at the end of our driveway and selling them, you know, like other people sell lemonade."

Jamie and Joe started laughing.

"Great!" said Jamie.

"What would you call it?" Joe asked. "You need a catchy name, make passersby slow down to read it. Maybe stop to buy."

"Cicada Sunrise!" Charles and Max said together.

"Cool!" Jamie and Joe said.

"I like that. And it works, as cicadas' songs get louder as their heat-absorbing shells warm up in the sun," said Joe.

"And in what ways would you serve them?" Jamie asked.

I bet she likes to cook, Max thought. "Well, actually, we've tried out a few recipes—sautéed in butter, dusted with spicy Old Bay, stir fried with fresh veggies . . . you know, Asian style."

"How about dipped in chocolate?" Jamie asked.

"Not yet," said Max. "Have you?"

"Oh, we have thought about it but not tried it. But I mean, you've actually eaten them? How do they taste?" Jamie asked.

"Not as bad as you'd think," said Charles. "But we remove the wings, as they don't seem to work as well as the . . . uh, bodies."

They talked about ideas for the Cicada Sunrise Stand

as they climbed many stairs and took the many steps over the stone-paved path closer and closer to The Morgue. And then they were there.

"Here we are!" Jamie said.

They were not far from Roland Avenue and what looked like a mini-shopping center, English Tudor–style buildings all linked together.

"It's the building on the end," Joe said.

They walked closer and closer, and then saw the end building. Big glass-front windows and a glowing sign that read Morgan & Millard, Drug Store and Luncheon Shop. On the old-fashioned door was a sign: OPEN.

"This is The Morgue?" Max and Charles asked together.

Jamie and Joe began laughing.

"Yep," said Joe. "The name is too long, so everybody here just shortens it to The Morgue."

"Come on, let's go in. I see some stools open at the counter. They have the best hot fudge sundaes ever!" said Jamie.

"Yes, guys, dessert time," said Joe. "And Grandma gave us money to treat you after making you sweat it out in the state of 'not knowing.' You did great."

"Yeah, you guys were brave and coolheaded," Jamie said.

They went into the bright, sweet-smelling shop and climbed up on the retro chrome, soft, red, vinyl-covered stools. Soon all four were eating vanilla ice cream covered in real hot fudge.

"Best ever!" Max said.

"One hundred percent," agreed Charles.

Chapter 13

Was It a Gray Ghost or a White Ghost?

After yummy sundaes, the walk back was just past sunset and lit by house windows and street-corner lamps. They felt their feet squishing cicada bodies like walking on honey—Joe had told them, "It's not rain but cicada pee, but it's OK because all they eat are tree juices"—and were totally enclosed by the surround sound of cicada songs.

It was almost nine when they arrived back at Grandma J.'s house. Parked in front they recognized Mom's van. Dashing down the sidewalk and up brick steps, soon they were on the front porch, united with Fred, Mom holding a sleeping Carrie, and Grandma J.

"We're enjoying the concert," Mom said. "I think it must be a lullaby, as Carrie went right to sleep only minutes after we arrived."

"How was walking on Sunset Path and The Morgue?"

Grandma J. asked.

"Perfect, except for all the bodies squishing under our feet," Joe said.

"And you'd be proud of Max and Charles. They were brave, didn't freak, and didn't even fuss at us when they found out about The Morgue," Jamie said.

"Oh, you pulled The Morgue card on them," Fred said. He laughed. "Was it good?"

"Best hot fudge sundae ever," Charles said.

"Yep," said Max.

"Grandma, you should hear the plan Max and Charles have," Jamie said.

"Yeah, very cool," said Joe.

"Oh, I bet I know," said Mom.

"Huh?" Fred said.

"The Stand Plan," said Mom. "We'll discuss it later."

Then it was time to go. All the many goodbyes were said. It was not like a final goodbye, but instead, plans were made for other adventures together soon. Moments later, the filled van was heading back home, away from Roland Park, towards the country called Caves Valley.

"Are we going to take Hillside Avenue?" Max asked.

"Of course," said Fred. "It's my favorite way." He turned the radio on and pushed a button to an oldies station: folk music, the Beatles, and all the sort of songs Fred and Mom liked to listen to when not in a classical music mood.

Max sat with his head against the door rest. He was feeling very sleepy. He closed his eyes. He really wasn't ready for any more scary things to happen.

Charles sat bolt upright. He was wide awake. The

waning moon sent eerie shadows down city alleyways, glittering and glooming on shrubs, through the tops of trees, and everywhere put him on high alert. He was really hoping the Ghost of Hillside Avenue would appear that night. A Gray Ghost or a White Ghost, which would it be?

The rolling gentle motion—up, down, and side to side—was a cradle rhythm that soon eased Max into sweet dreams of swimming down in currents deep, fins fanning, great tail sweeps. He was a monster-sized brook trout hiding in the shadows of his table rock, waiting for the right moment when the body of a king-sized, value-meal cicada would float by. Then he'd rise and float to the place, open mouth, and . . .

"Home, Max," said Mom. "Come on, sleepy guy, you need to climb out of the van, up the steps, and into bed. You're just too big to be carried like the sandman's bag of sleep."

"Uh, yeah," Max yawned. He rubbed his eyes. "OK, I'm fine, Mom." He rolled out of the empty van, closed the door, and headed into the house. "Night, Fred, great day. Night, Mom." He kissed her on her cheek, felt her kiss his, and headed up the stairs to the bedroom he shared with Charles.

Charles stood by the window, back to the room, face turned towards the world beyond their window glass.

"Hey, Charles. Hey, you OK?"

Charles turned to face Max. His big eyes looked bigger than ever.

"What's up, Charles, you look like you've seen a ghost . . . oh, man, did you?"

"Gray Ghost of a woman slowly coming through the trees, closer and closer, and as she came closer and closer, she turned whiter and whiter with what's left of this waning moon's beams going right through her until just an outline of her. And eyes . . . eyes looking at me . . . no, that's wrong. Eyes, her eyes looked right through me . . . through me as if she was seeing all that I am . . . all that I will be . . . all that I will ever be. Everything. She knew me, Max, and more. She let me know who I am. I mean, all this 'portal to nature' stuff Burt told us about. You guys all got it pretty quickly. Well, Jamie and you did. Joe took longer. But me, it didn't compute. It wasn't an equation I could figure out. It wasn't something I'd read about in any book I'd ever read, and you know I read. I read lots. No science teacher ever gave me an assignment like what Burt gave us today." He stopped to catch his breath.

"You saw the Gray-White Ghost and then you were somehow changed? Is that what you're saying?" Max asked.

Charles nodded his head. Then shook it. "Those eyes bored through me like an electric drill. Bored into my head and lit each and every one of my dim brain cells and I . . . I saw the light." He started to smile, and then he began to laugh.

"Man, Charles, crazy stuff," Max said. He sat down into a big, puffy bean-bag chair. "You saw this ghost and you think she zapped you?"

"Max, don't you get it? I saw this ghost. She looked into me and now I get it. Finally, I get it. My portal thing has to do with fire and light. Think about it. I can't stand to sleep and miss a sunrise. I love the sun in all the many ways we see it. The sun, Max, you know, is a huge gassy ball of fire sending heat and light throughout our solar system. I like anything light connected. Every evening, sunsets are a must and I miss them when clouds are like big curtains covering the sky. And yet, there's still some kind of light happening until night, and even then, unless it is a cloudy night, there are tiny star beams, which really are burning gas, powered by nuclear fusion, burning far, far away, some even from other galaxies. And then there's the moon, at all her many stages, reflecting the glorious light from our sun."

"Yep, I know. You always need to see sunshine, stars, or moonbeams," Max said and then thought, *yes, this is right on. Charles is a "light" person. A "lightweight" kind of guy. No, can't say that.*

"I wasn't afraid of her . . . you know . . . the ghost. She gave me answers and, crazy, I mean, it feels like she's set me in motion to somehow, someway, do something with whatever I ever do, but to do something that has to do with light stuff—fire, maybe—or to study space. Pretty cool, you think?" Charles said.

He's all aglow, Max thought and then said, "I'm happy for you, little bro, really, it's great. It's also kind of late. What time is it anyway?"

"9:48," Charles said after a glance at his lighted wristwatch. "Yeah, it's late, but I want to do something more before I go to sleep. Want to come, or are you too beat?"

"Well, I'm beat, but not. I'm more awake now than I

was before this enlightening story," Max said. "Or story of your enlightenment."

"Funny, Mr. Word Guy," Charles said. "OK, this is it. We sneak outside. We look and see if we can find any tree shadows on the ground. I know it'll be much harder than on a full-moon night, but I think we can find some."

"Then what?" Max asked as he squirmed out of the cozy bean-bag chair and managed to stand.

"You'll see," Charles said. "Follow me."

Quietly they went down the stairs, out the back door, off the deck, and onto the big lawn. Some cicadas were singing, but not like in Roland Park.

"OK, look here," Charles called.

Max saw where Charles was pointing. A shadow of a tree trunk and branches spread across the lawn, nearly invisible and yet there. Other trees nearby were fuzzy with freshly unfurled leaves of May, but this oak tree was dead. No leaves on it this year. Probably it would be cut down either this summer or early fall. Dried and seasoned, it would be used in their woodstove to help heat the house. But this May night, it was still standing with its shadow waiting.

"We're going to walk on this tree shadow, you know, the way we walk on balance beams in school. If we slip and fall off, well, we won't get hurt," said Charles.

"OK," Max said.

Under the black sky with only the moon but stars bright, Max and Charles walked on the shadow of a mighty tree. Carefully they placed their bare feet down, stepping slowly from the thickest part of the mighty oak out to its tiniest twigs. They took their time, attempting to follow every branch and many twigs until they both felt somehow filled and good and ready to be back inside. To sleep? Yes. To dream? Most likely. To remember this special day filled with brook trout, fly-fishing lessons, and special people in their lives? Yes, always. To also never forget how cicadas sing, look, smell, and feel? For sure.

★ ★ ★

Max and Charles had a full day and night back on May 31, 1987. It was a day and night that would change their lives forever as both grew, aging through their teens, twenties, and thirties, and into the men they were supposed to be. From this moment in time, they each began to understand what careers they were to grow into, using the element they identified as their portal into nature.

THE END

Epilogue

Only a trickle of water flows through the trout pools now, but it is clean and originates and spills from the Big Spring. Every spring, mint and watercress grow in and beside both pools and the spring.

Grandpa, Grandmas Y. and J., Mrs. Ellen, and Burt are all gone now, but their wisdom and stories, and the memories of them have not faded. Instead, with time, they seem to grow brighter and brighter as the phases of a moon change from eyelash to full every month.

Sadly, the Maryland Fly Anglers is no longer a large group helping raise wild brook trout, training youth to love all things wild in watery places. Some members still gather to talk fly-fishing talk. "Tight Lines!" is the wish they make to each other at the end of every little reunion. Many still tie Grey and White Ghost flies, sharing hackles, hairs, and threads as they compare and discuss how each fly should be flicked, fluttered, or dabbed on surfaces of deep river pools.

Roland Park waits for walkers on many trails away from road sounds and bustling busy-city crowds. If you are looking to enjoy a yummy hot fudge sundae at The Morgue, you will not find it there anymore. But a drive down Roland Avenue will take you to many places to eat, a great book shop, and excellent schools.

Like all children, Max and Charles grew up. They explored worlds and had many marvelous journeys.

The home in Caves Valley is now a place to drive by, stare at, wish, hope, and yes, to give thanks for childhoods filled with nature. It remains a place that offers gifts of learning who you are by entering special nature places through your own special portal.